D1003654

LOVE &
LOYALTY

by
Deborah Mayer

PUBLIC LIBRARY
EAST ORANGE, NEW JERSEY

A
Mayer

This is a work of fiction. The authors have invented the characters. Any resemblance to actual persons, living or dead, is purely coincidental.

If you have purchased this book with a 'dull' or missing cover-- You have possibly purchased an unauthorized or stolen book. Please immediately contact the publisher advising where, when and how you purchased this book.

Compilation and Introduction copyright © 2004 by
Triple Crown Publications
2959 Stelzer Rd., Suite C
Columbus, Ohio 43219
www.TripleCrownPublications.com

Library of Congress Control Number: 2005910631
ISBN: 0-9767894-2-6
Cover Design/Graphics: www.MarionDesigns.com
Author: Deborah Mayer
Associate Editor: Maxine Thompson
Typesetting: Holscher Type and Design
Editor-in-Chief: Mia McPherson
Consulting: Vickie M. Stringer

Copyright © 2005 by Triple Crown Publications. All rights reserved. No part of this book may be reproduced in any form without permission from the publisher, except by reviewer who may quote brief passages to be printed in a newspaper or magazine.
First Trade Paperback Edition Printing January 2005
10 9 8 7 6 5 4 3 2

Printed in Canada

PUBLIC LIBRARY
EAST ORANGE, NEW JERSEY
6125499396

DEDICATION | to Love & Loyalty

This book is dedicated to Aaliyah and Brooklyn.

ACKNOWLEDGEMENTS | First and foremost I acknowledge, praise and give thanks to the Creator through whom all things are possible.

To my mother and family, for your love and support, I thank you.

To my other family, Louis and Carmen Holmes, thank you from me and your son. We know it ain't been easy.

To Vickie Stringer, Lady Boss Supreme, thank you for the opportunity to shine. You will forever have our love and loyalty.

To Mia, Tammy and the rest of the TCP staff, thank you for smoothing out the bumps in the road.

To the many truly talented writers at Triple Crown, ya'll have set the bar high. May this contribution prove worthy enough to continue the trend.

To Shabaka Shakur, you know how we do boo, until you touch these streets again your baby girl has got you.

To my Nubian family Az, Nate, Anpu, Zulu, Wag and all the other brothas and sistas, this is our time, so let's do what we do.

To my girls, Debbie, Marilyn, Renee, Lillian, Trixcine, Vanessa, Nefer and those who this space doesn't allow me to mention right now, thank you for having my back.

Triple Crown Publications presents . . .

To my Hip-Hop family, "they fear what they can't understand, hate what they can't conquer." Thank you for bringing our culture to the world.

To the streets; the hustlers, balers, thugs, gangstas and playas repping their hoods, these are your stories written from the heart. Enjoy them, but pick up the jewels. We need to step the game up, only fools continue to fall victims to the same traps.

Love & Loyalty,
Deborah Mayer

P.S. Last shout out goes to Brooklyn Queen 'Lil' Kim now that's how you keep it gangsta ... much love and respects, the whole city's behind ya!

ONE | Javon took a deep pull, held it for a second, and then exhaled it slowly. He could feel the calm floating down on him. He held the blunt out, looking at it. Damn, this was some good shit … nice and smooth, the way he liked it. After taking another quick toke, he passed it over to E-Money, who was sitting on the passenger side of the ride.

Javon had a lot on his mind tonight. His eyes went to the rearview mirror, locking gazes with Derrick, who was sitting stoically in the back seat. Derrick disapproved of using drugs. Ironic when you consider he had no qualms about selling them. In a way, Javon agreed. Getting high could cause you to slip, and on the streets, even a small slip could lead to a hard fall. Still, every now and then, a blunt kept Javon from stressing to the point of insanity.

He took another pull and slowly let out a stream of smoke. He was hoping the blunt would help ease the tension in the air and break his unsettling thoughts. But as much as he tried to fight it, the weed did nothing more but heighten his sensitivity, almost forcing him to remember the run from last month …

Javon and Derrick rode down to Miami to pick up 10 kilos. After the 9-11 incident in New York, security was extra tight. You could see the National Guard at all the docks, airports and even at Port Authority. Sure, they were supposed to keep us from terrorists, but to a nigga in the game, all it did was make the price of drugs skyrocket. So much security meant drugs weren't coming to

New York as easily as before. That lessened the supply, but not the demand. When the supply can't meet the demand, the price goes up; economics 101. Even in the drug game, the same rules applied. In a moment of hustlers' brilliance, Derrick and Javon decided to head down South to cop. They knew Miami kept weight coming through its borders, and although security was up all over, it wasn't like New York; after all New York was ground zero.

They used their contacts to find a connect who could handle their order. They had to do their homework. You see, the thing about copping big weight is you have to deal with big money and shady people; that combination could prove lethal. As luck would have it the deal went down sweet, without any drama, or so they thought.

"Damn, that run was sweet," Javon insisted.

Derrick nodded as he looked in the rearview mirror wondering where the car with the girls, Nikki and Pam, was. *Maybe they took a wrong turn,* Derrick thought. *But how could they have done that, they practiced this ride a thousand times. Shit never changes and if you make a wrong turn, you call and tell us where you are.* "Javon."

"What's up?"

"Your phone ring?"

"Naw. Why?"

"Nikki and Pam. Where they at with the work?"

Javon turned around in a hurry, practically breaking the front seat with his knees. "Where the fuck they at, yo?"

"I ain't see when they turned off."

"The fuck?"

Derrick and Javon where somewhere between Maryland and New York when they last remembered spotting the girls. Derrick looked in the rearview mirror and it was official–either the girls got knocked or they had just pulled some slick shit.

"I knew we should've never trusted them bitches!" Derrick

pounded his fist, "Or that fuckin' G-man."

Nikki and Pam had to come to them through G-man, one of Derrick and Javon's trusted "workers."

When they arrived in New York to check G-man, he was no where to be found. The girls were gone, the drugs were gone and G-man was gone. It was all adding up to a big time double cross. It was a daring play but no matter how pissed Derrick and Javon were they had to give the trio credit for having the balls to play with their life.

G-man saw the chance to beat them for a nice lick and he took it. He and the girls were probably in B-more or DC right now, flipping their shit for three times what they would have gotten in New York.

"You know we gotta kill 'em right?" Derrick said coldly.

"Damn straight," Javon agreed.

It wasn't about the money. Even at the $15,000 they paid for each key, it wasn't going to hurt them too bad. But the fact is, they didn't believe in taking shorts of any kind, so sooner or later, they were going to have to deal with them, all of them. In the meantime they were determined to turn the tables on someone else.

Triple Crown Publications presents . . .

TWO | Marria was an exotic cocoa-brown. A Dominican beauty with long, thick, black hair and a body that made a man dream of sex, any man who saw her couldn't help but want her, and some were foolish enough to approach her. Marria was the wife of Manuel Cruz, so foolishness where she was concerned was costly. Manuel's jealousy wasn't because he loved her; she was merely a possession to him. He loved dominating her.

When he was coming up in the game, Manuel worked for her brother, Raphael. Raphael was wealthy, far beyond the ghetto standard. He had businesses both in America and the Dominican Republic. He had used his success in the drug trade to rise above the streets. Manuel learned a lot under Raphael and was loyal to him. In return, he treated Manuel like his own family. But when Manuel began showing interest in Marria, Raphael forbade it. Manuel, who was a proud man, was angered, yet he held his tongue.

For the next year, he continued to work for Raphael. He would see Marria often, but knowing he could not have her only made him harbor a quiet resentment for her. She never knew it. In fact, she had no indication of his true feelings. He would smile and treat her politely, but in his heart, he felt jilted. It was as if Raphael had declared him unworthy of her company.

Two years ago, Raphael was caught in a federal drug sting, one which Manuel had luckily avoided. Raphael and his crew were charged with a RICO indictment, and most of them were sentenced to life in prison. Manuel had quickly stepped in to take over, and just like the scene in Scarface, he showed up at Marria's house and took possession of her. Ever since that day, the little princess Raphael did not think he was good enough for was his to do with as he wished.

Manuel, or Manny as he was often called, was now one of East New York's major players on the drug scene. He enjoyed violence, money and women, in that order. His ruthlessness was the topic of many neighborhood rumors. How many of them were true, nobody knew or wanted to know.

Manny also had quite a number of girlfriends, a fact that was not lost on Marria. How could it be, when he did little to hide his indiscretions? Rumors, whispers and funny stares followed Marria wherever she went. Her only respite were the few stolen moments she shared in the arms of her "morenito," Derrick. Though Marria feared Manny, she looked forward to those secret visits with Derrick. He would spirit her off to his apartment and lavish her with the attention she never got at home. She loved the way he touched her, the way he made her feel special and the way he pleased her sexually.

Last week after they made love, Marria lay in the bed thinking about how much she enjoyed being with Derrick, and how she wished she didn't have to go back to Manny. Almost as if reading her mind Derrick turned to her, kissed her gently and said, "Run away with me, Marria."

At first, she thought it was a joke, but when she saw the look in his eyes, she knew he meant it. Somehow, her heart felt both joy and sadness. She wanted nothing more than to be with Derrick, but she knew that Manny would never let her go. She tried to explain to Derrick that it was impossible, but he refused to listen. He told her he loved her, and she loved him, so they would find a way. They made love again and talked again, and before they separated that night, they had devised a plan. All he needed was a copy of her house key and a signal from her on Saturday.

That was last week; today was Saturday. It was 11:30 p.m., and Manny was sitting in the front room of his East New York home, watching the television. Marria sashayed into the room wearing an extra large T-shirt and panties. She was aware of her effect on men, and tonight, she was depending on it.

Manny turned from the sports scores and watched her approach. She met his gaze, but said nothing. Instead, she took up residency in his lap. Manny held her in his lap but continued to watch the sports news. Marria, who had no intention of being ignored, leaned against him, rubbing his chest. She then began nibbling at his ear, licking it and snuggling her body closer to his. Though Manny's eyes remained glued to the television, his body began to give her the response she was looking for. She could feel him growing hard and reached down to massage his crotch.

"Mami, I'm watching the news," he told her.

"You want to watch the silly news or play with me?" she replied, while pulling the T-shirt over her head. Her breasts were perfectly shaped globes of brown flesh with dark nipples that stood erect, begging to be caressed.

"Damn, Mami, you feel hot tonight, huh?" Manny roughly grabbed her breasts, bringing one to his mouth to suck on her nipple. "You want Papi to fuck you tonight?" He slipped a hand underneath her panties slipping his fingers into her brutally.

"Yeah, Papi, I want you." Marria tried to sound convincing, though she felt like wincing at his rough pokes into her.

In an effort to distract him, she reached into his pants and began playing with his manhood. Manny gave a guttural growl as lust overtook him. He grabbed her panties and ripped them off her, and then, dumping her from his lap onto the couch, he began unsnapping his own pants.

"Not here," Marria said, quickly standing up and pulling him by the hand, "let's go to the bedroom."

Caught in the grip of passion, Manny followed her, undressing himself as he went along. Halfway there, she stopped. "You left the TV on," she said, turning back to cut it off.

"Forget it," he replied, not wanting to waste any more time.

"Go on, get undressed," she pressed him, "I'll be right there."

She sped off to the front room, turned off the television, then closed the drapes and walked back to the bedroom, all the while thinking of Derrick.

THREE | "That's it," Derrick said. "She closed the drapes.

That's the signal." They checked their guns, making sure there was a shell in the chamber, then they took the safeties off. They took two more seconds to make sure each of them was ready, pulled down their baseball caps, pulled up their coat collars and stepped out of the car, walking swiftly to their destiny. Each of them was dressed in black and carried a gym bag. They all wore gloves and kept their hands on their guns. Derrick had the house keys and also a silencer on his piece.

They hesitated outside the door for only a second. It was one of those seconds when you know in the next moment, things are going to go real good or real bad, and you hope for the best. Derrick tried the key; the lock opened. He turned the knob, opened the door and they stepped in. Sounds of Marria and Manny drifted toward them from the backroom. They swiftly locked the door behind them and began walking silently toward the voices.

When Derrick opened the bedroom door, Manny was completely naked, his face buried in between Marria's legs as she lay sprawled on their bed. Manny was surprised to see three black men in his bedroom with their guns pointed at him. He wiped Marria's cum from his lips and chin. Not sure of how quickly he should react he stared at the intruders and tried to study their vibe.

Derrick broke the silence. "Marria, you can get up now," he instructed her.

Marria got up from the bed, covering herself with the bed sheet as she made her way over to Derrick. At that moment, Manny, realizing her betrayal, leapt up in anger. His hands reached out toward Marria, but Derrick stepped in between them and brought his gun down hard on Manny's head. Manny crumpled to the floor.

"Good work, sweetheart," Derrick praised Marria. "Now, go help my friend."

Marria and E-Money walked out of the bedroom, leaving Javon and Derrick to deal with Manny.

"Manny, lay down on the bed with your hands behind you," Javon ordered.

Still somewhat in pain, Manny obeyed.

Javon gave his gun to Derrick, took out a pair of handcuffs he had brought with him, and cuffed Manny's hands behind his back.

"We know about the safe and we want the combination." Javon was hoping Manny would make it easy, but he didn't.

"Fuck you!" Manny spit back, "I'm going to kill you and that bitch!"

Derrick was not in the mood. He walked over to the bed, turned Manny over and pointed the gun at his knee. The silenced pistol softly spit a bone-shattering slug that pulverized Manny's right knee. The eerily quiet display of destruction was immediately punctuated by Manny's loud scream of agony. Javon had to cover Manny's face with a pillow to muffle the noise.

When he quieted down, Javon asked, "What's the combination?"

Manny was breathing hard, sweating profusely, and obviously in excruciating pain, but he remained silent. Javon looked toward Derrick, who stepped forward, pointing the gun at Manny's left knee. Manny's face gritted, waiting for the pain, but Derrick didn't fire. Instead, he let the gun travel higher, targeting Manny's family jewels. Manny's eyes widened with fear. He shook his head vigorously, eyes pleading with Derrick.

"The combination, Manny," Javon demanded.

This time, Manny reluctantly gave them the numbers. Javon walked over to the closet where he knew the safe was and tried the combination. The safe opened. Inside were seven kilos of cocaine, neatly stacked rubber banded packs of money and a black velvet pouch. Javon smiled.

When E-Money and Marria returned to the bedroom, they had filled his bag with jewelry and cash they had collected from around the house. Marria, who was now wearing a robe, looked toward Manny. She cringed at the sight of his bloody knee. A pang of pity struck her, but when she looked into his eyes, she saw pure hatred staring back. The look Manny gave her sent chills through her body. She subconsciously began to move toward Derrick, who as naturally as any father would protect his own child, put his arm around her. Javon filled both Derrick's and his bags with the drugs and cash. They gave the bags to Marria and E-Money to set by the door.

As soon as they left the room, Derrick turned to Manny and shot him twice in the face. The large caliber slug took half his head off. Marria returned, and seeing Manny's decimated features, stood there transfixed by the gore.

"Don't look." Derrick quickly turned her away from the sight. He sat her on the edge of the bed. With her back toward what was left of her husband, he tried to console her. Derrick knelt before her, speaking in soothing tones.

"Derrick," Javon interrupted, "get her dressed and let's go."

"Go ahead, we'll catch up," Derrick replied.

Javon left the room and went to help E-Money carry the bags out to the car.

"Don't feel bad; I'm here with you," Derrick told Marria. "Remember all our plans? We can make them come true now."

Marria began to calm down and come back from her shock. "That's right," Derrick encouraged her. "Just forget about this, close your eyes and think about our future."

Marria closed her eyes and a smile began to form on her face as she thought about herself and her morenito. Derrick kissed her softly on the forehead, then stood and shot her clean between the eyes. Marria never saw it coming. Derrick hoped she died happy. E-Money and Javon were already in the car when Derrick trotted up the block, opened the car door and jumped in the back seat.

"Where's Marria?" Javon asked.

"Resting in peace," Derrick replied.

Javon thought he heard a trace of sadness in Derrick's voice. He was going to say something, but instead decided to let it go. He turned the key, heard the engine come to life and drove off.

FOUR | Javon opened the front door. It was early morning. The sun forcibly invaded the interior of his home. It was a bright Monday morning–in fact, too bright for Javon, who wasn't a morning person. Usually, he didn't get out of bed until nearly noon. Today was different. He had to meet with Derrick.

The move two nights ago had gone down smooth. By now, the car they'd used was in Benny's chop shop, dismantled into many pieces. All their clothes had been burned to ashes, and Derrick's gun had been taken apart and tossed out over the Brooklyn bridge. There was nothing to tie them to the incident.

"What's up, homie?" Javon stepped aside to let Derrick in.

"Same old two step," Derrick replied, handing Javon the morning paper.

"What's up with you?" Derrick asked.

"You know my struggles." Javon closed the door.

They walked down the hallway, turning when they got to the basement door. Javon's basement was like a men's club. It had a pool table, farther toward the back, a hot tub, and toward the front, a lounge area with a large screen TV, a surround sound system and a well-stocked bar. The wood paneling and dim lights made it a perfect place to relax.

"What's the word?" Javon asked.

"It made the papers," Derrick replied, "the bodies were found yesterday, but the cops haven't got any suspects."

"What's the word on the streets?" Javon asked, turning to the story in the newspaper. He knew word on the street was usually more accurate than what the police knew.

"Nobody's sure what went down. Manny had a lot of enemies."

Javon read the newspaper in silence. Derrick reached over to the end table, and grabbing the remote, began channel surfing, finally settling on BET.

"Damn shame," Javon absent-mindedly mumbled.

"She had to go," Derrick replied, knowing intuitively who Javon was referring to. "Once people would have seen her with us, they would have put it all together. We couldn't afford that."

"I know."

And that was the problem; Javon did know. He knew even before he went into the house, but he left the call up to Derrick. That still didn't erase the blood from his hands. This life was funny like that. Violence was acceptable when the target was a participant. Every hustler, stick up kid, or gunslinger understood each day could be their last. That's why they lived fast and played hard. It was part of the mentality of live for today, fuck tomorrow; it wasn't promised anyway.

It was different when civilians got caught up in the mix, though. A hustler's wife and kids were supposed to be kept out of the game. In the old days, it was almost an unwritten rule, but nowadays, beefs were sometimes settled at your doorstep, with a person's family as collateral damage. That's when you realized how brutal this game could be. Javon didn't like unnecessary violence. Violence always begets more violence, and he knew sooner or later, it would come for him.

Javon closed the paper and sat back, watching the TV screen. There was a half-naked video dancer bumping and grinding to the music. That's how she made her money. He couldn't knock her hustle. Everybody had a hustle and that happened to be hers. For Javon, hustling was in his blood. His thoughts shifted, and he began to think of his mother. Mama Williams was a dark-skinned, West Indian woman. She was born in Jamaica and spent her youth working to contribute to her household finances.

When she turned 20, she made the trip to New York, hoping to better her circumstances in the land of plenty, America. Though a smart woman in many respects, when it came to matters of the heart she proved to be young, naive and easily infatuated; in no way a match for a 24-year-old high-yella, slick-talking street hustler named Tony. Pretty Tony is what they called him.

Tony had a way with women that was pure magic. He met Mama in 1976 and the rest is history. Plenty of women warned Mama that Pretty Tony had a wandering eye, and probably more body parts than that to keep in check. But you can't tell a woman anything wrong about a man she loves.

Mama swore that no woman would ever take her man. Unfortunately, she was right. In 1977, only a month after Javon was born, Pretty Tony was shot dead, trying to loot a liquor store during the blackout. Mama initially struggled with the grief that his death brought, and then struggled with the reality of being a single parent. For years, that reality brought Mama untold sorrows. Even more so, since Javon was the spitting image of his father. Every time Mama looked in Javon's face, it reminded her of the love she had lost.

Over the years Mama did attract a few other men. Though she was a good woman, each new suitor resisted the temptation to stay. To most men, a woman and child was like a chain and ball; a responsibility to be avoided at all costs. Mama and Javon struggled on, surviving partly on welfare and partly on the part-time jobs Mama would find.

Javon was seven years old by the time Mama met Raheem, and things changed. Raheem had knowledge of self. He understood his role as a black man and he valued family. More importantly, he adored Mama. Moving into their household, he became the man of the house. He emphasized education, always pushing Javon to do better in school.

"These devils want you to be illiterate so they can master you," he would explain. "You have to beat them at their own game."

Javon hadn't had a father figure to help him make sense of things before, so he appreciated the strong example of manhood that Raheem brought. So did Mama. Things were good for a long while. The only dark cloud on the horizon was Raheem's desire for a child of his own.

Mama never conceived any more children. Raheem tried not to make a big deal of it, but over time, it ate away at him. It wasn't that he did not love them; in fact he treated Javon like his own son. Nonetheless, he was a man who believed in family and wanted a biological child of his own. It didn't help that Javon was light-skinned. Mama and Raheem were both dark-skinned, and the contradiction between them and Javon always brought questioning looks from strangers.

After seven years things changed. Raheem didn't slack in his responsibilities or ignore Mama, but little things were different. They would argue over nonsense, and sometimes, Raheem would disappear all night without explanation. They still loved each other, but staying in love was hard.

Then one day, lightning struck twice. Mama lost the second love of her life when Raheem died in a car accident. He had fallen asleep behind the wheel of his car. As if his death in itself was not bad enough, the news got worse. Raheem had been returning late from the house of another woman; a woman who happened to be the mother of Raheem's one-year-old son, Razohn. Javon was fourteen then, and old enough to understand the pain that Mama felt. In some ways, he knew she blamed herself. Her inability to give Raheem the children he wanted caused him to roam.

"I gave E-Money $15,000." Derrick's voice shook Javon from his retrospection.

"Huh?" Javon was lost for a moment. "What you say?"

"I gave E-Money $15,000," Derrick repeated.

"Oh yeah, that's good."

"What do you think of him?"

Javon liked the kid. He was dependable and had been with them for two years. Though he was just 20 years old, he was wise for his age.

"He's fam," Javon said. "Why, what's up?"

"You know the operation we been setting up down South?"

"In North Carolina?"

"Yeah, well, I was thinking about putting the kid in charge down there."

Derrick started flipping through the channels again. Javon thought about what Derrick was trying to do. Derrick wanted to send the kid out of town just in case somehow, word got out about Saturday's move. By putting him in charge of North Carolina, they had someone they could trust down there, so in the end, it was killing two birds with one stone. E-Money would see it as a promotion since he would be getting more money and running his own crew. Everybody wins all across the board.

"Sounds like a good idea," Javon agreed.

"I'll kick it with him later today."

"Listen, the seven bricks will last about two weeks," Javon commented, changing the subject. "We also got $350,000 in cash and some ice."

Javon walked over to the bar. Behind it was a large floor safe, where he'd stashed the loot from Saturday. Javon opened the safe and grabbed the small black velvet bag. He brought it over to where Derrick was sitting and tossed it on the table in front of him. Derrick opened the bag and examined the contents. He let it spill out onto the coffee table. Fifteen large-sized diamonds sparkled in the light from the TV.

"These are top of the line," Derrick said, looking at Javon.

"I went by Ruben the Jew's house yesterday and he priced them at about $15,000 apiece," Javon informed him.

"That means they're really about $20,000 a piece."

"Yeah, that's what I was thinking," Javon agreed.

"When did this cat come up like this?"

That was a good question. Manny had taken over Raphael's operation and he was balling, but not nearly to the extent that Raphael had been. This much coke, cash and ice seemed out of his range. They had pegged him for about $100,000 in his safe. Instead, when you add it all up, they had almost eight times that in loot. It just didn't figure.

"Anyway," Derrick said, handing the bag of diamonds back to Javon, "what you got for me?"

Javon took the bag and walked back to the safe. Placing the diamonds back in the safe, he took out two kilos and wrapped them in a brown paper bag, then dropped them into a plastic shopping bag and returned to where Derrick sat.

"You coming through today?" Derrick asked, standing up and grabbing the bag from Javon.

"Probably later. Page me if you need me."

They walked toward the stairs and started to climb out of the basement. As they reached the top of the stairs, they could hear the sound of R. Kelly's latest joint bumping through the house, which meant Peaches, Javon's newest jump off, had arrived.

Javon glanced at Derrick. He knew from the frown on his face that he wasn't quite feeling Peaches. "What's the look for, Dee?"

"Yo, it's that broad, I can't stand her. For real I can't."

"Why?" Javon questioned. "She's cool people. And she don't stress me and shit like some of these other chicks."

"Yeah?" Derrick raised his eyebrows, "All I'm saying, son, is to keep both eyes on her ass. Make sure she don't mistake you fuckin' her for you lovin' her. We don't need no bitch messing up shit. Feel me?"

"It's all good, Dee, trust me."

"Ai'ight, I'm out." Derrick made his way to the front door.

"One," Javon replied as he watched Derrick head for his truck.

Peaches was sitting on the sofa, rolling some weed.

"Hey, Shorty," Javon said as he walked past her on the way to the bedroom. Javon picked up the phone and called Craig, one of college friends, at his office.

"Keynote Management, Mr. Thomas' office, can I help you?"

"Hi, Lori, this is Javon. Is Craig in?"

"Oh, hello, Mr. Williams. He's in the office; I'll put you through."

"Thanks."

A few seconds later Craig was on the line. "Javon?"

"Yeah, I got your message."

"Hey, what's up, buddy. I want to see you Friday. I got something for you to see," Craig informed him.

"What time?"

"Can you meet me at Sweetwaters at seven-thirty?"

"Sure, I'll be there."

"Okay, see you then." Craig hung up.

When Javon stepped back into the living room, Peaches was in the middle of the floor, dancing, eyes closed, toking on a blunt and grooving to a Mary J. Blige remix. She had on his Stephon Marbury Knick jersey, which fit her like a mini-dress, just reaching mid thigh. Below that was the sexiest pair of legs he'd ever seen. Cream-colored, slightly bow-legged and beautiful all the way down to those ankle-length, white sweat socks she had on. With no makeup and dressed like she had just rolled out of bed, her hair in a scarf, she still looked good enough to give Halle Berry a run for her money.

Javon went to the kitchen, got a carton of orange juice out of the fridge and came back and just watched her move. Life had its pleasures and she was one of them. As the song faded into the next, she opened her eyes and found Javon watching.

"What you looking at, sexy?" Peaches said, flashing her mischievous smile.

"A dream come true," Javon answered. He was always amazed at how sexy this girl was. She slid up to where he was standing, slipping in between his arms, her head pressed against his chest. This was her space; she had commandeered it six months ago, and over time, it had claimed her as well.

"Well, what kind of dream was it?" she asked, playfully.

Javon took the blunt from her and took a deep pull. Letting the smoke out, he bent and whispered in her ear. "It's the one where I lick you from head to toe."

"Mmmm," she moaned, grinding her hips against him. "You sure it's just a dream?"

His little man started to stand up firm. Javon placed the blunt between his lips and reached down with both his hands to cup that incredible ass of hers. She wasn't wearing any panties. He gripped her by the ass and lifted her up. She wrapped those beautiful legs around his waist and he carried her into the bedroom. Life had its pleasures and Javon intended to enjoy one of its sweetest.

FIVE | Peaches was feeling good tonight. She'd left Javon's place at about 6.00 p.m., which gave her enough time to make it to her place, get her gear together and then drive up to the Bronx. Peaches had taken last night off, but today was Friday, a big money night, and she had no intention of missing out. And she knew Hunt's Dolls would be packed with niggas ready, willing and able to give up their cash; all she would have to do is flash a little ass and shake some titties in their face.

As Peaches stood in her dressing room in front of the mirror, making sure everything was looking right, Sandra came strolling her way. Sandra was her girl, the only one in the club she really fucked with.

"Your boy Tamel out there," Sandra informed her. "He's sitting at the bar, sipping a thug passion."

"Good, I can use the paper," Peaches replied.

Tamel was one of her regulars. He was an up and coming hustler whose paper was starting to get long, and Peaches was in his pockets, taxing that income.

"Girl, the way that nigga paying out, you need to stop playing games and hit him with some of that coochie before he find another hoe."

Sandra checked herself out in the mirror. Sandra was the only girl in the club who could turn as many heads as Peaches did. Sandra was brown-skinned and built like a brick house; thick in all the right places. She swung both ways but respected the fact that Peaches was strictly dickly.

"Shit, the little nigga's already open, if I gave him some pussy, he'd be following me around like a lost puppy. I definitely don't need no young ass nigga all up under me," Peaches remarked.

"Bitch, you ain't right," Sandra responded, laughing and high fiving Peaches' audacity.

"Yeah, but I definitely ain't wrong, either."

Sandra walked over to her purse to get a cigarette and then proceeded to light it up, in total disregard of all the no smoking signs plastered all over the dressing room. She walked back over to Peaches, continuing her spiel.

"If it was me, I'd throw some of this thing on his trick ass and take all the paper."

"That's because you're desperate!" shouted one of the other girls getting dressed.

A round of laughter followed the comment.

"You're going to be desperate to get my foot out of your black ass," Sandra retorted.

The laughter quickly died down. Sandra was cool, but everybody knew she had that side of her you didn't want to see.

Turning back to Peaches she lectured, "You know, a young nigga ain't a bad thing; they got strong backs and can get it up four or five times a night. Just teach the little nigga how to eat some pussy and you straight."

"I already got a nigga that does all that and I don't have to teach him nothing." Peaches smacked Sandra on the ass and walked into the club.

"Don't be bragging, bitch 'cause I ain't forgiven you for that shit, either!" Sandra yelled after her.

The lights were dim, but Peaches saw Tamel as soon as she stepped out. He was no longer sitting at the bar, now he was sitting at his regular table. Tamel settled himself and prepared for his dick to be rock hard. He eyed Peaches as she walked out. Peaches made her way across the room. A few of the guys tried to get her attention, but Peaches told them all to hold their money, she'd be back. Closer to Tamel's table, another guy grabbed Peaches' wrist, holding out a ten spot. She could tell Tamel was watching her, so she decided to give him a show.

"Ten dollars?" she asked the guy who stopped her.

"Ain't that what a lap dance cost?" he asked, bewildered.

"Yeah, if you want one of them girls to do it for you." Peaches stretched her arms outward, letting him see the other girls. Then she turned for him, slowly giving him a view of her money maker as it jiggled before him. "If you want all this ass on your lap, you got to come better than that."

To seal the deal, she bent over a little, made it drop and bounce like she was hitting switches on a low-rider. By the time she turned back around, he had pulled out a fifty. Peaches smiled, took the cash, then worked him something proper.

Before she left him, she bent to whisper in his ear, "Remember to always ask for Peaches."

"Peaches," he repeated, mesmerized.

"Next time, it will be even hotter. I promise." She left the table and made her way over to Tamel.

"Hey, Sexy," Peaches greeted him.

Tamel didn't reply. He just stared at her with an attitude. She turned around and started to walk away. Peaches had only taken two steps when Tamel reached out and grabbed her arm.

"Where are you going?" he asked, annoyed.

"Let my arm go." He did, and she started to walk away again.

"Peaches!" he yelled, giving her the evil-eye. She stopped and turned to face him.

"What's your problem?" he asked.

"What's YOUR problem?"

"You had me waiting on you," Tamel complained.

"So?" Peaches was staring him straight in the eyes. They both stood like that for a few seconds, neither wanting to back down. Then Rory, the bouncer, came over to check on the situation.

"Peaches, everything all right?" he asked.

"Yeah, everything's cool; this my nigga, right?" Peaches asked Tamel, her eyes never leaving his.

"Yeah, everything's cool," Tamel replied.

Rory, not completely satisfied, stood around for a few more minutes until he was sure there weren't going to be any problems.

Meanwhile, Peaches had stepped closer to Tamel. Her body was inches from his. She knew this made him uncomfortable. Most men, Tamel included, wanted to be in control. Peaches being this close to him made him uncertain. Part of him was excited, her physical presence enticing him, yet her attitude warned him not to touch. That's what Peaches wanted. She wanted him to realize that no matter how much he wanted her or how close to him she might be, she was only his to have when she decided, and only for as long as she decided. Sometimes, you had to treat a man like a child to get him to act right. Sometimes, you showed him the candy, but didn't let him have it. Other times, you let him taste it, then take it away. Eventually, they got the message. Today would be Tamel's day to learn these valuable lessons.

"Now, you want to tell me why you acting all the fool up in here?"

"Ain't no big deal."

"Oh, no, you done made it a big deal, so tell me what's up."

"It's just that you know I come in here every Friday just to see you. I don't even fuck with none of these other bitches; I come straight to the back and wait for you, but you got me sitting here like a fool while you all up in that nigga face." He looked at her sincerely. "I know it's your job, but I be showing you mad love; the least you can do is come check me, let a nigga know you acknowledge his presence."

That was the problem with these niggas. They would tell you

they understood it was just a job, then in the next breath, wanted you to treat them special. Hustlers were the worst. These are the niggas that supposed to know the game, respect the rules and shit, but they acted as bad as the lames. Peaches' rule was to never explain the game to a player; he's supposed to know. When a player steps out of pocket, you check him hard. If he's true to the game, he'll respect the lesson. If he's not, then cut the nigga loose. Players come and go, but the game never changes.

"Stand still," she told him. Then she turned around, pressing her rear against him. She took his hands and placed them on her hips, letting her ass tease him until his erection was straining against the front of his pants. When she had him good and hard, she walked him back to his seat. A few curious eyes watched them, which didn't faze her, because Peaches loved a crowd. She sat him down, then took her place in his lap, straddling him face to face. She reached down into his pants and arranged his hard on where she wanted it. Then she straddled it. She had on a G-string, though it must have felt to Tamel like straight pussy on bone. She rode him gently, looking in his eyes. She pleased him the way she knew he wanted. Tamel's breathing became heavy with delight.

"You like that?" she asked salaciously.

"Yeah." Tamel was enjoying the attention.

"Now, don't I make you feel good?"

"Yeah, Peaches, you make me feel real good." His eyes closed and Peaches could tell he was on the verge of wetting himself.

"Tamel?"

"Yeah, Peaches?" he moaned softly.

"Open your eyes and look at me." When he did, Peaches stopped humping him, bringing a halt to the pleasure he was feeling. She looked him in the eyes, and with the same sincerity he had given her, she spoke to him. "I can always make you feel good, but Tamel, if you ever catch an attitude with me again, I will stop fucking with you all together. Do you understand me?"

Tamel heard, but had no response.

"Do you understand me?" she asked again, the seriousness undeniable.

"Yeah," Tamel answered, feeling defeated.

"Good, then tell your baby you're sorry."

"I'm sorry, Peaches."

Peaches smiled, knowing he would not cause any more problems.

"That's my nigga." Peaches held him close, her body against his, and whispered in his ear, "Grab my ass."

He did, and she humped him until he ruined his pants.

SIX | Sweetwaters was a nice little restaurant on the upper West Side. It was a cozy spot that made the customers feel at home. There was a small stage where performers could entertain. As Javon drove there, he threw on a CD he had recently bought by Goapele, a new singer out of the bay on the West Coast. The new crop of singers coming out had a style that was bound to change music for the next few years. Talent was making a resurgence. Alicia Keys, Jill Scott, Vivian Green—yeah, music was going back to being something special. Javon cruised and grooved all the way to the restaurant.

When Javon reached Sweetwaters, it was already 7:30 p.m. The place seemed a little crowded. Then again, it was a Friday night, and that's when the weekend warriors come out in droves. Javon asked for the Thomas party and was escorted to their table. Craig was seated with two other people. The one he recognized was Jackie Green, Craig's lawyer. She had also helped him on some business matters a couple of times. Javon shook hands with Craig, greeted Jackie and was introduced to the third person, a gentleman by the name of Charles Jackson. He was the owner of a small, independent record label. Craig introduced Javon as the owner of Club Paradise.

Though Craig knew there were some darker aspects to Javon's activities, he never asked, never intervened and never acknowledged anything except that he was "Javon Williams," the Club's owner.

27

Craig and Javon met during college. They both attended Norfolk State University. There was only a small group of New Yorkers there, so most of the time, they stuck with each other. Craig and Javon also played ball together. Craig had a wicked jump shot and Javon had that quick first step that got him to the basket every time. On the weekends, they partied.

Before college, Craig used to DJ with a crew in New York. In fact, his crew was pretty well known. Even in the clubs they'd go to in Virginia, a lot of the DJs had heard of them, which helped Javon get into a lot of private parties he wouldn't have been able to attend otherwise.

During their sophomore year, money was tight, so Craig started promoting parties. He showed Javon the ropes and together, they threw parties that had people coming from as far as Atlanta. By the end of the third year, Craig was the man to see when it came to putting an event together. Not only would he promote jams, but he'd find acts to perform and even DJ himself.

Though things began to look up financially, all the extra activities took their toll on Javon's grades. To make matters worse, Javon's mother was diagnosed with cancer. It was still in its early stages, so the doctors felt optimistic about her recovery. Still, Javon was not about to let her go through it alone, so he dropped out of school and went back home to New York.

Javon kept in touch with Craig, but didn't see him again until two years later when they bumped heads at a party he had sponsored. They reminisced and talked about doing something together. By that time, Javon was deep into the game and hungry to get into something legit. Craig helped him open the club, no questions asked. He even set up a few events to make sure it got off to a good start. It did, thanks to Craig. Club Paradise now had a regular clientele. It was a mature crowd; business people letting their hair down on the weekend type of crowd, which was cool with Javon. He already had enough drama with his other activities; he didn't need a wild ass Hip Hop club to worry about.

They sat around sipping their drinks. Javon could tell Charles didn't have any idea what they were meeting for. Craig was like that; he always played his hand close to the chest, and he revealed things at his pace.

As they waited for the food, they shared industry chit-chat, who was hot in the music world and who wasn't. They were in the middle of a conversation about Beyoncé , whether she really had talent or just a great body and a hell of a promotion team, when the featured artist came out to perform. She was a dark skinned beauty with locks wrapped up a la India Arie style. Her eyes were captivating, with long dark lashes that accentuated her face. Her lips were thick and exotic. You could look at her and mistake her for Naomi Campbell. Physically, she was stunning, at least Javon thought so, and she reminded him of how good Kenya Moore looked in the movie "Trois."

She held the microphone and started her piece in spoken word. It was like some of Jill Scott mixed with the depth of Lauryn Hill and flavored with a dash of spicy Sonia Sanchez. Then, out of the blue, she sprung into her melody. Her voice thundered from her body, low and husky. Seductive, yet emotionally charged. She sang of love, betrayal, sorrow and redemption. Her sound floated on air and surrounded the listener, wrapping around them like a warm blanket on a chilly fall day. Passion ruled her, and everyone was drawn into her aura. Her spirit caressed the crowd like an attentive lover. When she sang her last note, everyone in the restaurant was spellbound. A wave of applause shattered the silence. She bowed and walked away from the microphone.

"She's good, huh?" Craig asked.

"She's great!" Javon responded.

Charles agreed and wanted to know who she was. As if in answer to the query, she walked over to the table.

"This is Fatima Amir." Craig stood to make introductions.

When all at the table had been introduced, they brought her a seat and Fatima joined them.

"People," Craig stated, "this is my latest client. The new star on the horizon. "He beamed proudly.

They all knew he had good reason. There was little doubt that she had star quality talent, which made everyone all the more curious to hear why Craig had gathered them there. If it had to do with this new talent, it could prove profitable.

For the next two hours, Craig laid out his business ideas. They ate, drank and went over his master plan. By the time the check arrived, they were all highly impressed and wanting a piece of the action.

SEVEN |

Peaches was in the dressing room counting her ends when Sandra walked back there after her set. Sandra was looking so right in her outfit that Peaches had to give her props.

"You turned it out tonight," she complimented Sandra.

"Not like you, freak. You was working that floor like it wasn't no other girls out there tonight," Sandra replied.

"What other girls?" Peaches asked, jokingly.

"I know that's right." Sandra laughed. "What's up with Tamel?"

"Same old shit; another trick trying to tell me how to do me."

"I know you set that nigga straight."

"For sure!"

It didn't matter if it was in the club or on the outside, niggas always thought if they tossed you some ends, that gave them the right to make demands on you. Some women were stupid enough to accept that bullshit, but not Peaches. She understood the game better than most. To Peaches, it wasn't about the money, that's where so many people had it twisted. It was about pleasure. Hustlers made money so they could spend it on things that brought them pleasure. Money wasn't the prize. It was only the currency that got you closer to the prize.

Everybody's prize was different, but Peaches knew you could always tell what it was by what people spent their money on. Niggas who came in here and spent their money on her let her know that the prize they wanted was her body. Not her, just her

31

body, because they didn't know her. It was just the body that they saw and wanted. So, Peaches rented it to them. Never did she sell it, or let them control it. She knew as long as they didn't own the prize, they would continue to pay the price for it. And whenever a nigga started acting like he did own it, she took it away. You either learned to play by her rules or not at all; most chose her way. That was the lesson Tamel had learned today.

For the rest of the night, Tamel sat there and watched as Peaches went from table to table taking currency for a prize nobody would ever own. When she was done, she returned to his table, sat in his lap and soothed his ego. After all, he was her best paying customer.

EIGHT | Last year, Craig started managing a young rapper by the name of G-Rydah. The kid had skills and street appeal. Handled right, he was destined to be the next Jay-Z or 50 Cent. Craig used his know-how and influence to gain the kid a solid underground reputation in the clubs and on the mix tape circuit. He was shopping the kid to the major labels, looking for a lucrative deal. Unfortunately the music industry is a cut-throat business. Most major labels have an in house management team and do their own artist development and promotion.

Though Craig was known in the industry, he refused to ally himself with any one major label. He didn't want to give up too much control to some stuffed shirt that only cared about the bottom line. Music executives were about the money; they didn't care about the music. They pimped the artist into making trendy radio friendly fluff to sell records and would drop an artist quickly when they were no longer profitable. Craig had seen it done dozens of times. Yet, not being affiliated with a major label limited Craig's resources.

About six months ago, another manager named Brian Russo, who did work for a major, tried to snatch G-Rydah away. Russo offered G-Rydah a record deal and a cash advance, but G-Rydah had to switch managers. In spite of all that Craig had done to get him this far, G-Rydah saw the big times calling and wanted out of his contract with Keynote Management. Craig could have fought it in court, but fighting to keep an artist that wanted out was always bad for business. No matter how it turned out, you always came out looking like you were trying to hold an artist back from fame and fortune. Craig didn't want a reputation for being one of those managers that artists couldn't trust.

He was set to sell the kid and cut his losses when he mentioned the situation to Javon one night when they were hanging out at Club Paradise. Javon advised him to be patient and give it another couple of days. Javon discussed the matter with Derrick and the two of them came up with a plan.

Two days later, Russo and G-Rydah were in a Midtown parking garage when they became victims of a New York City mugger. Russo was shot during the robbery. Though it was not fatal, he was hospitalized for a week. G-Rydah, who had witnessed the shooting first hand, was scared, but not as much by the shooting as by what the shooter said.

The gunman shot Russo first, then, turning to G-Rydah, commented, "Loyalty is important. Turn your back on those who helped you, and you'll be seeing me again. Keep your mouth shut and do the right thing."

The gunman then proceeded to rob G-Rydah and Russo before getting away. G-Rydah may have just been a studio gangsta, but he was smart enough to know good advice when he heard it. When the cops came, G-Rydah couldn't remember the robber's face. The cops cleared it as just another incident in the big city.

The next day, G-Rydah went to Craig's office and announced he was staying with Keynote Management. Later that week, Javon received a card in the mail. It was unsigned, though Javon knew the handwriting. Written on the card was one word: THANKS.

The experience made Craig realize that he was vulnerable. He couldn't expect the big boys to play fair when it came to trying him for his artists. So, that night, Craig started formulating his plan. In the last six months, Craig had signed an R&B group that had good potential, and now, a sure fire hit in Fatima. Armed with the right pieces, Craig was ready to put his plan into effect. He had done the homework.

Charles Jackson was a black man who had been in the business for 20 years and had a solid reputation as a fair man. He owned Triumph Records, a company with a few good artists, mostly jazz and alternative R&B funk. None were marquee artists, but all were serious musicians with talent and a small fan base. Triumph was good enough to acquire a decent distribution deal, but not big enough to draw any really big-named artist to the label. Their resources for promotion, video and artist development were strained. Charles could have come under a major label; quite a few would have welcomed him, but like Craig, he prided himself on his work. He believed in putting out good music and that's what impressed Craig the most.

Craig planned to join forces. A merger would give each the needed boost to take them to the next level. Craig would be bringing to Charles' label a number of good artists. Three that were sure chart toppers, as well as his own undeniable skill and talent as a promoter. This was precisely what Charles needed to pump fresh blood into his company and put him on a level to better compete with major labels. It also worked to Craig's benefit by insuring that his artists would get a record deal at a reputable establishment. To round it off, Craig had added Javon as the third partner.

Javon was the one with the money to invest. He had the deep pockets and the venue. In any business, money made the task of operating that much more easier. But, in addition, Javon had a club that was a tremendous plus. It meant a sure venue to showcase the company's talent before taking them out on the national stage. Since New York was a tough audience, the club would provide an opportunity to gauge an artist's appeal in front of some harsh critics. Like the saying goes, "If they could make it here, they'd make in anywhere." It was also good business for the club. This was the plan Craig laid on everyone at the restaurant. It was a good plan and everyone seemed to like it.

Although Craig never mentioned it, Javon knew there was another reason he wanted him aboard. By bringing Javon on, Craig knew sharks like Brian Russo would have to feed somewhere else. What Craig didn't know was Javon was looking for an opportunity like this. It was his ticket out of the game.

NINE | The phone was ringing. Fatima could hear it vaguely though her mind was still in the fog of sleep. She reached it over and picked it up, hating to get out of bed.

"Hotep, sista," the voice on the other end greeted her.

"Hotep," Fatima replied, groggily.

"Fatima, I know you ain't still in bed." It was Aaliyah, Fatima's best friend and confidante. "You're going to be late for services."

"What time is it?" Fatima asked, trying to shake the sleep.

"Girl, it's 10 a.m. You want me to come pick you up?"

"Yeah, I'll be ready by the time you get here."

Last night, they had all listened intently to Craig's ideas, Fatima as well, since her future was tied to any decision they made. They had discussed the details, asking questions along the way. Fatima could sense everyone liked the proposal. Then, the light-skinned brotha, Javon, invited them all to his club, so they left the restaurant to go party.

Club Paradise was down in the SoHo section of Manhattan. To some artists, SoHo was the avant-garde Mecca. To most others, it was the hub of alternative lifestyles, everything from art and music, to clothing and sexuality. Club Paradise fit in perfectly with its surroundings. The building itself appeared to be a refurbished warehouse, and although spacious on the inside, you didn't get the sense of vastness you would have imagined. Instead, Club Paradise had that home grown local club vibe, where it seemed everyone knew each other.

The house DJ was good. Craig had recommended him, and as usual, he was right. He played mostly R&B, some funky dance tracks and sometimes smooth, laid back joints, depending on the crowd's responses. Every now and then, some modern jazz tune or commercialized Hip Hop would help to change the pace. Overall, it was a good scene and a good crowd.

Fatima and all the rest of the group arrived around 11:00 p.m. and stayed until 3:00 a.m. By the time she got home she was exhausted and crashed out. She really wanted to sleep the day away, but with all the slack she had been getting lately, she knew she had to go to the service.

She got up and jumped in the shower, turning the water slightly cooler than usual to snap her out of la-la land. It was working; the cobwebs were clearing.

After washing up she oiled her body and then her locks. She kept a special blend of oils for her body and another for her hair. The mixtures of oils were all natural and specially blended for her by this sista out in Bed-Stuy, who specialized in natural herbs, oils and aromas. Fatima couldn't stand perfumes. She hated those women who would walk by and leave their perfumed scent hanging heavy on the air for hours. Fatima had her oils created to bring out her own natural scent; the subtle scent of a woman.

Fatima wrapped up her locks, then threw on her black beads and her garments. She was just about finished by the time Aaliyah pulled up. It was 11:30 when she stepped out the door. As they drove, Fatima filled Aaliyah in on last night's events.

"Well, do you think this is your big break?" Aaliyah asked while she glided through the sparse Saturday morning traffic.

"I don't know, Liyah," Fatima replied, wondering the same thing herself, "but I do know I get a good vibe from these people. Anyway, this week they want me to record some vocals for G-Rydah."

"The Rapper?!" Aaliyah asked excitedly.

"Yeah."

"Damn, Fatima, he's famous!"

"He's not famous yet, but it is a big opportunity."

"He's been on BET and MTV, that's famous enough. You going to do a video with him?"

"I guess so; I'm not sure. Liyah, I'm just glad to finally be back in the mix after all the bullshit I've been through."

"All I'm saying is, don't forget me when you're famous," Aaliyah said seriously. "I always knew you were going to be famous one day."

From your lips to God's ears, Fatima thought.

Triple Crown Publications presents . . .

TEN | It was Sunday night. Derrick and Javon were in Javon's basement watching a WNBA game. The cops hadn't come up with anything on the homicides yet, but they were shaking down all the drug spots in the East New York and Brownsville sections of Brooklyn. Most of the spots Derrick and Javon had were in Brownsville, and since the cops were making it too hot to get any real money, they told the crew to shut down and take the night off. Don't get it twisted, the drug business is just like any other business. It's all about the Benjamins, but sometimes in an effort to make a dollar, you stood the risk of losing ten; that's when smart hustlers stepped back.

Both Derrick and Javon understood the value of being patient. Shutting down for the night might cost them money, but in the end, it would be less then what they'd spend on bail and lawyers if they stayed open. That was a jewel a lot of hustlers ignored—every dollar ain't worth chasing. So, instead, they were sitting in Javon's basement watching Tameka put her foot in the Liberty's ass and drinking beers.

"The Liberty are just like the Knicks," Derrick said, "always coming up short when it counts."

"Stop hating," Javon remarked between sips of his beer, "the Knicks are rebuilding right now and you can't even front on the Liberty; they got a good team, even without Weatherspoon."

"Yeah, they're good enough to beat the Knicks, but it's the Comets and Sparks they got to worry about," Derrick laughed.

"Ha, ha," Javon said sarcastically. "You missed your calling. You could have been a comedian."

"Don't blame me if they make it so easy."

"You want another beer?" Javon asked, getting up to grab another bottle from the mini-fridge.

"Nah, I'm good." Derrick leaned back, enjoying the game.

Javon returned to his seat. Though he was watching the game, his mind was on the conversation he'd had with Craig. Javon saw it as a way to put an end to his hustling days and still be in position to make money. He definitely wanted to put Derrick on it.

In their time together, they had both made money and been there for each other through the good times and bad. Javon wasn't silly enough to think he knew the game better than Derrick. Still, he worried about him. While Javon had taken some of his money and bought a club, Derrick didn't own anything. He didn't even own a house; he simply had apartments all over New York and New Jersey and nobody ever really knew where he rested his head at night. Maybe this would help him.

"Yo, Dee, you remember my man, Craig?"

"Yeah, the music cat, right?"

"Yeah, him. Check it, he's getting ready to put something together and he's putting me on to it. It's a chance to jump into the music industry."

"And do what? What you know about the music industry?" Derrick asked, looking at Javon like he was crazy.

"Not much," Javon admitted, "but I'm getting down with some cats that do know. So what's up? You want to roll with me on this or what?"

"Nah, that ain't my thing, homie. Anyway, what the fuck would I do in the music industry?"

"Nothing, that's just it, Dee, we can sit back, do nothing and make money."

"I'm already making money," Derrick informed him after taking a sip.

"Yeah, we making money, but look at the risk we taking to make it. Dee, we done had a good run, but you know this shit never lasts forever. Everybody takes a fall sooner or later. Right now, while we on top, we can step out the game and blow up legally on some music shit." Javon tried to sell Derrick on the idea.

"Jay, there are risks in any business that deals with money; you can't get around that. Besides, homie, in the music business, them cats don't have any morals. They just a bunch of thieves without honor."

Javon was dumbstruck by that last statement. A gun slinging drug dealer talking about morals and honor. "You got to be kidding," he said, looking at Derrick in disbelief.

"Nah, homie, I'm dead-ass serious. The business world is all about the money. They don't give a fuck about you or me. Yeah, I know it seems when we getting that paper out there, that we on the same shit, but we ain't. What we do ain't about the money, as much as it is about what he money gives us."

"Oh yeah? And what's that?"

"Freedom, for one. Most of us ain't never had the opportunity to enjoy our lives. How many motherfuckers you know done grown up in the hood, poor as hell, and even now, when they grown, they still on welfare or working for some minimum wage that don't even make it through to the next paycheck? Imagine the stress of living like that day in and day out. Not knowing where your next meal will be coming from. Don't get me wrong, niggas been living like that forever, so we know it ain't going to kill us, but damn, son, that shit is a burden on a nigga's mind. When we out there hustling, we out there making the money to get rid of all those burdens. And you know what? We doing it for self ... feel me? We don't have to kiss nobody's ass for that paper, like no bullshit ass job. That's the closest thing to freedom we ever going to see.

"The second thing," he continued, "is that this game gives us is respect, homie. The foundation of all this shit is respect. Money gets you power and power gets you respect. That's the truest shit them rap niggas ever said."

"Dee, you the same nigga who said you don't respect half the niggas in the game, now," Javon reminded him.

"That's 'cause half these niggas nowadays is ass!" Derrick was getting animated. "These niggas nowadays ain't no real hustlers, and they damn sure ain't no gangsters. There're rules to this shit. You know the code of the streets and too many motherfuckers done forgot that. Let me ask you something. Would you fuck with some snitch-ass nigga?"

"Not if I knew he was a snitch."

"Right, 'cause you know it goes against the code we live by. And what if one of our comrades got knocked, would you take care of him?"

"Of course."

"And if one of our comrades gets shot down, what we going to do?"

"Retaliate."

"Fucking right! And check it, what if all you had was a dollar and I needed a dollar, how much could I get?"

"I'd give you my last dollar, homie, and you know that."

"Yeah, I do; that's the love and loyalty and that's what I respect. Let me tell you something. Money don't mean shit. We ain't never had no money from the start, so we know how it is to be dead-ass broke, and we know how to make something out of nothing, feel me? If we lost it all tomorrow, we'd make it back the next day. But it's not like that in the business world. When them niggas lose their money, they go home and shoot their brains out. They'd rather die than live without money, that's how important that shit is to them. They don't give a fuck about nothing or no one, it's each man for themselves. Now, how could you fuck with niggas like that?"

"I feel what you're saying, but even on the streets, you got niggas that think like that. I done seen plenty of niggas that go against the grain and don't respect the rules of the game," Javon reminded him.

"That's true, but those are the niggas I'm saying don't deserve any respect. Those the niggas that when the opportunity arises, we get them for everything. Yo, it's either niggas accept death before dishonor, or we impose death after they go and dishonor shit. Justice is brutal, but at least in this game, it's served. Now, where you going to get justice when they rob you in the business world ... the courts? Man, them cats got the best lawyers in the world. They'll rob you, then make robbing you legal and fuck justice. Justice, like loyalty, in their world, is sold to the highest bidder."

Javon had to admit that Derrick made a lot of good points. He decided to leave the subject alone and finish watching the game. Later, they shot some pool and by 10:30, Derrick was making his way to the door. After seeing him out, Javon went back down to the basement, fixed himself a brandy and jumped into the hot tub to think.

Sometimes, it amazed him how differently he and Derrick saw things. Derrick lived for the streets, thrived on it, trusted it and understood its idiosyncrasies better than Javon ever would. To Derrick, the streets were the end. To Javon, the streets were only a means to the ends. Yet, for all their differences, the two of them had a bond that was unbreakable.

Derrick and Javon met back in 1997. Javon had come back to New York to care for Mama Williams, who was undergoing chemotherapy for cancer. The bills were stacking up and Javon was having a hard time finding a job that could put a dent in them. He thought about promoting parties like Craig had taught him, but the music scene was too chaotic. Biggie had just been killed and an East-Coast, West-Coast war was forming, making parties the place NOT to be. With his options looking limited, Javon turned to the drug game. Crack was dying in New York. The anti-drug effort was in full swing and the cops were coming down hard on drug dealers. Most hustlers were going out of town to make their money.

Considering how many people Javon knew in Virginia from throwing parties, he figured he could cop some coke in New York, slip down to Virginia for a few days and make enough to pay his bills. Javon started copping ounces and bouncing back and forth between NY and VA. But the coke was half-assed and inconsistent. He was getting more complaints than anything else. That's when Javon got plugged in to Derrick.

Derrick had only been on the set about a year, but he was quickly gaining a reputation as the man to see for good coke. Javon started dealing with him and business started picking up immediately. By being plugged into the club scene in VA, Javon still had access to a lot of the private parties that went down. He was pushing two or three ounces a night working the party circuit. The best part was that they were mostly private parties, which lessened the chances of bumping into any undercover police.

Before long, Javon was pushing close to a big Eighth each weekend. He thought he was big time, but Derrick saw his inexperience and took Javon under his wing. He showed Javon how to set up drops, find runners and mules and how to create a buffer between himself and the business, while at the same time expanding things. In less than a year, Javon was spending less time actually dealing with the product end of the business, yet making five times what he used to. That's when they became partners. Javon was amazed at the depth of Derrick's knowledge, considering Derrick was only two years older than he was. As he got to know Derrick better, he came to understand why.

Derrick came from a family of hustlers. His father was an old-time hustler who died of a drug overdose when Derrick was still young. After his father's death, his mother and older brothers took over. They were all deep in the game, with operations spread throughout the East Coast. Derrick always knew he was destined for the drug game, but when he was seventeen, he got arrested for an assault and weapons charge and everything changed. His mother, not about to let her youngest child go to prison, paid a top notch lawyer to make the case disappear. Then she sent Derrick to the military to learn some discipline.

Derrick served Uncle Sam for three years. By the time he returned, his entire family was also serving the government, except in their case, it was in the Federal prison system. The Feds had arrested everyone, including his mother. The Feds really wanted their connect, but no one, not even his mother, would ever disrespect the game by snitching. So they all got life without the possibility of parole. Home, with no money and a family in prison to support, Derrick turned to the only thing he knew: the drug game.

Now, seven years later, he was still as committed to the game as ever.

As for Javon, he was tired of the grind.

Triple Crown Publications presents . . .

ELEVEN | Peaches rolled over, looked at the clock and

yawned. It was noon, and she was just getting up. Streams of sunlight were sneaking in through the picture window in her bedroom. Her high rise apartment was located on the bright side of the building and she was thankful because the other side faced a brick wall.

The weekend had been good. She pulled in about $3,500 for three days of bumping and grinding, which meant she could afford to take the next few days off. She definitely had to see Nana this week and take her some money. Damn shame, as fast as it came, it went even faster. Not much she could do about that; at least her bills were paid up.

Peaches stretched lazily, then got up and went into the bathroom to shower. Once in there, she decided to fill the Jacuzzi instead, and relax. This was one of the benefits of being a stripper—she made enough money to enjoy some of life's finer things. While the water was filling she went into her dresser drawer and pulled out her stash of weed. She grabbed a blunt and her lighter off the dresser, walked back into the bathroom and sat on the edge of the tub to roll herself a fat one. Two minutes later, she was neck-deep in scented water, enjoying a much needed rest.

She pulled on the blunt and let her mind drift. She thought about the bullshit she had to deal with this weekend. Saturday night, when she went to work, the manager had the nerve to call her into his office to beef about her behavior the night before. He told her he didn't like the way she was carrying on in the club.

"Excuse you?" Peaches snapped at the owner. "Do you have to be reminded that I'm the best bitch up in this hole in the wall, stank-ass piece."

"Peaches—"

"Don't Peaches me, shit! Most of the chicks here are as exotic as the hoes on the strip. Saggy tits, cellulite asses, and sporting more scars then niggas on Riker's Island."

The owner didn't say much, after all Peaches was right and he knew in order to stay afloat he needed Peaches, more than she needed him. After all she was the main reason customers came to this dump in the first. She had more regulars than anybody else in the place. So she let him know that if he had a problem with her, she could always take her ass over to the Pussycat Lounge. She was sure they wouldn't have a problem with her working there. The nigga got the message and backed up off her.

To tell the truth, she didn't like working all the way up in the Bronx. She basically came up there to put distance between her work and her daughter. If it weren't for Tiffany, she would have stayed in Queens. There was probably more money in Queens anyway, 'cause except for Tamel, the guys in the Bronx didn't pay out like she wanted. Stingy-ass niggas want to stick their fingers all up in your pussy for a fucking dollar.

Tamel was another problem in itself. The boy had it bad and was starting to act up. Peaches had to smile at the thought of Tamel. He was kind of cute. He was always talking about taking care of her, and damn, the way he looked at her made her hot.

Some girls would cry about how they hated dancing, but not Peaches, she loved it; it gave her a chance to explore her sexuality. To look in a man's eyes and know he wants you that bad, turned her on. Sometimes she felt like a goddess, like every man was meant to worship her. She felt irresistible. The first time she understood that feeling, she was only 13 years old. Back then, her body had matured far past her age. That's when Peaches, her mother Suzy Q, and Troy, Peaches' big brother, all lived together in Queens.

Troy was four years older than Peaches and their dad had left Suzy Q shortly after Peaches was born. He simply traded her in for a younger version. He barely came around to see his children, and he never gave them any money unless Suzy Q threatened to take him to court. Troy was trouble; there wasn't any other way to describe him. By the time he was 17, he had already been to Spofords twice and Riker's once.

When Peaches was growing up her family lived on welfare and whatever Troy brought to the house. Suzy Q was 35, but still a good looking woman, and she kept a handful of boyfriends to help pay the bills. Sometimes, when it was quiet, Peaches could hear Suzy Q and her boyfriends in her room. Suzy Q may have let them enjoy her body, but she would check them quickly if they got too demanding. Arguments were an everyday event.

As for Troy, he and his hoodlum friends never went to school. When the welfare caseworkers started bugging Suzy Q about finding a job, she went to work in a bar and left Troy to watch the house, which he turned into a hangout. He would have a hookie party every day and fill the house with teenagers smoking weed, drinking beer and sneaking off to the rooms to have sex. By the age of seventeen, Troy already had two kids by different baby mamas.

Troy's partner was a boy by the name of Bobby. Bobby always watched Peaches. He was the first one she caught doing it. He was careful not to let Troy see him, 'cause partner or not, Troy had a bad temper. Still, Peaches would always catch him watching her out of the corner of her eye. He especially liked to watch her ass. So, Peaches would tease him sometimes and walk around the house wearing a T-shirt and panties when she knew he was around. She got a thrill out of watching Bobby try to sneak a peek

51

when she would walk by. Of course, Troy would send her to her room.

One day, when Peaches was thirteen and had just come home from school, Troy and Bobby were in the staircase getting high. She had to go upstairs, so she tried to squeeze in between them. As she did, her rear brushed up against Bobby, and when it did, he kind of humped her unnoticeably. But Peaches did notice it; she even noticed the little smirk on his face when he did it. She went to her room, thinking that if Bobby wanted to play games, she would, too. Peaches took off her jeans and put on a light fabric dress without her panties on. If Bobby tried to hump her this time, it would feel like she had nothing on.

She started down the stairs, squeezed between Troy and Bobby, and once again, Bobby pushed his hips out to rub up against her. This time, when he did it, she stopped right there, with her ass up against him. Then, she stopped and started asking Troy for five dollars. Troy, who hated being disturbed when he was getting high, wasn't trying to hear her. Still, she stayed there, switching her hips so that Bobby would get the full effect.

He got nervous and tried to back away, but the wall was behind him and he had nowhere to go. Peaches backed up further, really rubbing it up against him, and making small circular motions with her hips that Troy couldn't see, but she knew Bobby was feeling. In no time, he had a hard-on he couldn't hide. That's when Peaches walked away, leaving him exposed. He sat down quickly, hoping that Troy hadn't seen him. Peaches didn't want to get Bobby in trouble, but she wanted him to know she was on to him.

When Peaches went to bed that night, she had thoughts of Bobby. She could remember the feel of him hardening up against her, and it made her feel special. Peaches knew even if he wanted to, he couldn't stop it from happening. She could do it again; in fact, she could make him feel like that any time she wanted, and that knowledge made her feel in control. That was the first time she understood the power she had over a man, and in the weeks and months that followed, she made a game of teasing Bobby when she could get away with it.

Returning to her present thoughts Peaches finished smoking the blunt. The water was getting cold, and she was both hungry and horny. The hunger she could take care of herself. As for the horniness, she got out of the tub, walked over to the phone and dialed Javon's number.

"Hey, sexy," she greeted him.

"Hey, shorty, what's good?"

"You. I need my fix, can I come over later?"

"I ain't got nothing planned; come on over and we'll hang out. Do you have to work tonight?"

"Nope, I'm all yours."

"Good, then I got you all to myself tonight."

"Javon."

"Yeah?"

"You my nigga, right?"

"And you knows this."

"What's your favorite dessert?" she asked.

"Come on, baby, Peaches and Cream, of course," he responded.

On the other end, Peaches smiled.

Triple Crown Publications presents . . .

TWELVE | Derrick drove through the block, scanning for
unfamiliar faces. A lot of people took the way Derrick moved for
paranoia, but he didn't care. He knew this wasn't a game, like so
many had taken to calling this street life. Everything out here was
serious and deadly. You survived by staying a step ahead of everyone else. Derrick made sure he was always on point and always
had a way out. It was always that one thing you missed that would
come back to hurt you, so he tried not to miss a beat.

It used to be you could spot a cop a mile away. They just stuck
out like sore thumbs, but not nowadays. Now, they had cops who
were born and raised in the hood. These niggas had the walk, the
talk and the mannerisms down to a science. Derrick didn't waste
time trying to figure out who was or wasn't a cop. He lived by one
simple rule: if he didn't know you weren't a cop, then you were a
cop. Better safe than sorry.

Derrick turned the corner, parked and walked back up the
block satisfied nothing was amiss. As he reached midway up the
block, he saw Red steering the customers toward the building.
Inside the courtyard was a hustler named KB and an unknown
nigga slinging in front of the entrance.

Derrick and Javon had a number of spots they supplied.
Though they had enough runners and pickup men, Derrick still
liked to pass through the spots periodically to make sure things
were running smoothly. It helped to keep him in touch with the
flow of the money, first-hand.

Right now, he was upset with KB and Red. This was basically a new spot—they had just opened up six months ago. KB was told to hustle out of the apartment on the second floor. Derrick didn't like them out in the open. A lot of crews did it like that, but Derrick was more security-minded.

Ignoring the nigga he didn't know, he stepped to KB and told him, "Let's go upstairs."

Derrick entered the building, quickly followed by KB. The unknown nigga got up and followed them.

"Only KB," Derrick pointed. The kid stared back at Derrick, barely disguising his displeasure.

Derrick had the impression the kid had done some time. It wasn't his stocky build, or the way his hair was waved that gave him away, it was his eyes. Niggas who had done time didn't screw up their whole face when they shot you an intimidating glance. Ice grills were for amateurs and clowns. Niggas who had mastered the art of intimidation did it with their eyes and maybe just a slight cocky smile that said it all. That's the way this kid was staring at Derrick, now. Derrick had every intention of calling his bluff, but Red walked through the door.

"What's up, Dee? I wasn't sure if you wanted me to keep sending the customers in or hold them up."

"Forget them for now, I want to talk to you and KB upstairs." Once again, ignoring the other kid, Derrick started making his way upstairs. KB and Red were close behind. Once inside the apartment, Derrick closed the door and turned to them.

"Who the fuck is this nigga downstairs?"

"His name is Killa and he lives on the block. He just came home from Upstate and he was looking to get on, so I told him to steer some of the people he knows my way and I'd look out for him," Red explained.

"Oh, yeah? So how do you know the nigga is trustworthy?"

"We ain't giving the nigga the drugs to hold. We just figured since he lived on the block, he knows who all the fiends are. I was just waiting for you to come around so I could introduce him to you. Son is legit; he's just trying to get on his feet. You know how it is when a nigga just come home."

Derrick couldn't believe how naïve these niggas could be. Derrick didn't think the kid was 5'O, but that wasn't the only foreseeable problem. The nigga was probably a stick up kid, trying to feel out their operation and these niggas were stupid enough to give him a blueprint, if not the key to the front door itself. It wasn't that Derrick was against looking out for a nigga just touching the streets after doing a bid, but he wasn't taking anyone on face value. Just cause a nigga was in the mountains, didn't mean shit. There were plenty of fool-ass niggas doing bids.

"If y'all want to fuck with him, y'all responsible for him. Give him some ends and let him stay on the outside steering or looking out, until we check him out. Don't put the package or the money in his hands. I don't want him in the apartment for any reason, got that?"

They both nodded in agreement.

Derrick continued, "And KB, I told you before to stay off the street."

"I know, but Killa was showing me the fiends, he knows all the heads on the block." KB's explanation only angered Derrick more.

"So, this nigga already changing up the program?"

"Nah, it ain't like that; he just knows the hood better than me, and the fiends come flocking when they see him."

"You think fiends give a fuck about who serves them? The fiends come to whoever got the best shit. When that nigga was up north, they were coming to cop from you, and if you're not here, they'll come to cop from the next nigga. So don't get it twisted. A fiend's loyalty is to the bag, no one else. Anyway, did Rock come through to pick up already?"

"Yeah," they informed him in unison.

"So, y'all straight for now?"

"Yeah we straight," responded KB.

Derrick made his way out the door, leaving KB in the apartment. Red followed him out. Downstairs, the kid, Killa, was waiting on them.

As they reached the first floor, he approached them.

"Yo, son, could I get a word with you?" Killa asked. Derrick, who already had his hands in his pockets, gripped his gun, though he didn't pull it out.

"Yeah, what's up?" Derrick responded.

"I been out here helping your little homies push their shit on the block..."

"And?" Derrick had no intention of holding a conversation about drugs with some nigga he didn't know from a hole in the wall.

"And, it's just that a nigga recently came home and I'm trying to eat, too, feel me? I see y'all doing y'all thing. I ain't trying to step on no toes or nothing. I'm just looking for some work."

"Where were you at Upstate?" Derrick asked.

"I came home from the EL."

"Yeah, who was in the EL with you?"

"A few niggas, but I was mainly solo bolo. I ain't with the crowd shit. Anyway, fam, what's up? Can a nigga eat or what?"

Derrick looked him in the eyes, trying to figure out where this nigga stood.

"KB and Red will get at you," he informed him, then made his way down the block. Derrick's homie, Wag, was doing time in the El also known as Elmira Correctional Institution. Derrick made up his mind to put out the word for Wag to give him a call so he could get some inside info on Killa.

As he made his way to his Navigator, Derrick's thoughts went to the conversation he had with Javon the other night. Derrick understood Javon's desire to get into the music industry, but he just didn't want any parts of it. Every nigga with some paper was trying to squeeze their way into the music industry, and that, in itself, was a problem. Sure, Javon was smart, but there were a lot of stupid niggas out there with paper. It wouldn't be long before one of them got into the music industry and fucked up bad enough to have the Feds checking everyone's background. If Derrick knew nothing else, he knew one thing for sure: a hustler had to avoid the spotlight, 'cause no matter how good you clean up, there's always that bit of dirt that you missed. Javon was putting himself on stage, and sooner or later, the spotlight was sure to shine.

Derrick reached his car, got in, and put the key in the ignition. When he turned it, the engine came to life, and with it the radio blasting ironically enough G-Rydah's mix tape banger, "Gangstas Don't Die." Derrick pulled off, wondering how much truth there was to that.

Triple Crown Publications presents . . .

THIRTEEN | Peaches lived in Queens on the South

Side, about a forty-minute ride from Javon's house in Flatbush, Brooklyn. For the last six months, she'd been making that trip about three times a week. Funny thing is, when Peaches first met Javon, she thought he was just another pretty boy. She and Sandra had taken a day to go shopping on Fifth Ave., and that's where they first met him.

"Girl, look at that fine-ass nigga over there," Sandra said.

Peaches turned to see who Sandra was talking about and there he stood, a light-skinned, six feet, two inches tall and well put together brotha. He didn't have a big muscle-bound body but he wasn't slim, either. He was a good 220 lbs. and well defined like a model. Face wise, he was a pretty boy, one of those Ginuwine types.

Peaches hated pretty boys. Sure, they were good to look at, but most times, that's where the value stopped. Pretty boys were used to girls throwing themselves at them all the time, so they never had to work for the pussy. As a result, their skills were usually half-assed. Most couldn't hold a decent conversation, and only a few were any good in bed. Some were so into their looks that they acted like girls. She had dealt with enough pretty boys in the past, and each time, Peaches made it her business to break them.

"He's okay," Peaches replied.

"Girl, please, that nigga's fine as hell," Sandra insisted.

Peaches did check him out again, and she had to agree, he was fine. He stood tall and looked strong. He was about twenty-something, she would guess, which put him in her age group. He dressed in that expensive quality, yet slightly understated style. The look you got when you weren't dressing to impress, but you impressed anyway.

"Yeah, he's fine," Peaches admitted, and went back to looking for the jeans she wanted.

They were still looking through the racks when Pretty Boy entered their section of the store. He checked them out and smiled. *He has a cute smile*, Peaches thought to herself, but she didn't want to encourage him, so she kept on shopping. Sandra, however, with her fast ass, had also seen him smile, and responded with a wink. Peaches gave her one of her "knock it off" looks, but it was too late; Pretty Boy was already on the way over.

"Good afternoon, ladies."

"Good afternoon, yourself, sexy," Sandra responded.

Peaches said nothing.

"My name is Javon; I hope I'm not disturbing you."

"Nah, baby, my name is Sandra and this is my friend ... "

"He doesn't need to know my name," Peaches stopped Sandra, then, turning to Pretty Boy, she said, "you are disturbing us. We came here to shop, not meet guys."

"Girl, why you bugging?" Sandra countered.

Peaches made a quick mental note to check her later for flipping on her in front of some stranger. Before she could continue to put Pretty Boy in his place, he backed up.

"It's okay, Sandra, she's right. There's a time and place for everything, and this is obviously the wrong time, so we'll talk when the time is right."

Pretty Boy turned and walked away. Peaches watched him leave, feeling a little disappointed that he didn't put up a bigger fight. He hadn't gotten angry, nor had he apologized. He simply accepted the situation and excused himself. Sandra, on the other hand, was upset with Peaches, and let her know it.

"What the fuck you do that for?" Sandra exploded.

"I didn't know he was going to take off like that," Peaches explained. But Sandra wasn't trying to hear her.

"What did you expect, Peaches? You jumped down his throat for saying hi."

"Well, go chase him if you want!"

Peaches was getting upset with Sandra. As many men as she had sweating her, here she was, acting like she was starving for a nigga she didn't even know.

Sandra looked his way, and for a second, Peaches thought Sandra was actually going to chase him down. She was relieved when Sandra turned her head and went back to picking through the racks.

Half an hour later, they had their choices and made their way to the checkout counter. Once there, a clerk motioned them to the side. He opened up one of the empty registers and started ringing up their purchases. When he finished, he passed Peaches a receipt stamped PAID. The receipt was on a store account with the name Williams. Peaches considered not saying anything and walking out with the purchases, but with her luck, she knew she'd be half way out the store when they'd come after her with the police. She had no intention of being embarrassed out here today, so she spoke up.

"Excuse me, there's been a mistake, my name is not Williams," Peaches informed the clerk.

"No mistake. Mr. Williams asked that you two ladies' purchases be put on his account," replied the clerk.

"Mr. Williams?" Peaches asked, still confused.

"Yes, and he left this envelope for you." The clerk handed Peaches a small white envelope, then continued to bag their purchases. Inside the white envelope was a small note which read:

Ms. No Name, please allow this shopping day to be on me. It's the

least I can do for disturbing you. I would like to get to know you, I hope you will allow me the opportunity. When you find the time, please call me.

It was signed Javon, and had his number at the bottom.

Sandra was eyeing Peaches suspiciously. Peaches rapidly stuffed the note in her pocket and told Sandra to grab the bags so they could get out of there before they made them pay for the stuff. It took a week for Peaches to call him. Although she hadn't wanted him to, he had impressed her. They spoke on the phone, met for lunch and felt each other out. Peaches told him she was a stripper. She didn't say dancer, she said stripper, and she wanted to give it to him raw. He didn't seem disgusted like some men or excited like others. He just accepted it as a regular job. He didn't ask what club she worked at, a sure sign he didn't want to come see her. So she didn't invite him. He didn't mention the purchases he paid for. She was waiting to see if he would throw it up in the conversation, but he didn't. She gave him some points for that. He never asked Peaches if she had a man. Instead, he kept the conversation on her, gave her his full attention, and complimented her enough to let her know he appreciated what he saw.

What Javon didn't say with words, his eyes said for him. Still, he was cool about it. Peaches was starting to like the attention he gave her. The way his eyes made promises and his smile gave assurances.

Their lunch lasted about an hour, maybe a little longer, then he had to leave. He asked her if she needed a lift. She didn't, so he paid for her lunch, walked her to her car, gave her a kiss on the forehead and left her standing there. His last words were, "Give me a call when you have time, okay, shorty?"

Peaches drove away angry with him. She was impressed, curious and wanted to see him again. She enjoyed his company and the attention he gave her. Peaches wanted more, but he never asked her for her number or asked to see her again. That's what

made her angry. Peaches could see it in his eyes, she knew he wanted more, too, but he was trying to play it cool. She didn't have time for the games, so she decided not to call him.

That week, Peaches couldn't stop thinking about him. Every nigga Peaches knew wanted to get with her, and here this fool was trying to act like he could care less. The following week, he was on Peaches' mind so much that she was even thinking about him at work. That was the last straw. She didn't want to be rubbing up on some nigga while her mind was stuck on another nigga. That type of shit only made her horny, so the next day she decided to put an end to the games. She was going to call this nigga and put this thing down on him so proper that when you looked up the word "pussy-whipped," you'd find his picture, name and address. That night, Peaches called Javon.

"I want to see you," she told him.

"Sure. When?"

"Tonight."

"You want to go out tonight?"

"No, I want to come over tonight." She hesitated only for a second.

"Do you want me to come pick you up?"

"I can drive. I just want to know if I'm invited."

"You're invited."

He gave Peaches the address. That was the first time she made that trip; now, six months later, she was still making that trip on a regular basis. Looked like he was not the only one whipped. The thought made Peaches smile.

Triple Crown Publications presents . . .

FOURTEEN | When Fatima walked into the studio, a
fog of smoke clung to the air and the pungent smell of weed was
strong enough to make her gag. A bass-heavy Hip Hop beat was
playing from someone's boom box, as about ten young, black men
stood around passing blunts and bottles of Olde English. Most
had on sweat suits or jeans sagging halfway off their backsides.
None looked older than twenty, yet all looked like they were sea-
soned veterans of the street. A few heads turned to take notice of
Fatima's entrance, but most were too caught up listening to G-
Rydah and another brother trade verses.

Fatima looked around for Mr. Thomas or any of the adults she
expected to see in control of the session, but none seemed to be
around, so she pulled up to the crowd and listened to the brothers showcase their skills. G-Rydah was good, but the other brother was definitely holding his own.

Hip Hop was like that. It was about competition and pride. It
was born in the streets where most black people had nothing. The
average person living in urban America had little education and
even less money, and though vocational skills were limited, the gift
of gab was an art form. If you could shoot the right words at a sister, or game a vic out of his money, you were the man on the
streets. That's why pimps and hustlers were so idolized by many
ghetto youths. They were the masters of that gift. Yet, the epitome
of the art form was in the world of Hip Hop. Young brothers and
sisters who mastered the lyrical gift of gab were becoming mil-

lionaires and international mega-stars.

Sometimes, it was amazing to think about. A pastime that had started in the school yards of poverty-stricken neighborhoods in the South Bronx was now a global phenomenon that could be found in the villages of Africa, Brazil, Jamaica, Europe and even Japan.

"Who you be?" asked one of the guys standing by Fatima.

"I'm Fatima. I'm supposed to be doing some work with G-Rydah."

"Yeah, they said he's supposed to be doing a re-mix." He looked her up and down, trying to gauge what she was about. "Yo, Gee! Shorty here's the one that gonna blow on your track!" he shouted over to G-Rydah.

The lyrical contest faded and Fatima became the new focus of attention.

"You Fatima?" G-Rydah was now questioning her. "Craig says you the hottest thing since Mary J Blige."

"I can do a little something," she responded, not wanting to sound boastful.

"Well, let me hear something," he pressed her.

Fatima hated to be put on the spot like that, but she knew from past experience that the only way to meet a challenge was head on. She dropped her bag, lifted her head and let go of her voice. Fatima started with Alicia Keys' joint, "Falling," then slid into a little Faith Evans, then to Carl Thomas' "Emotional," to showcase her range, then ended with a Mary classic, "Reminisce." By the time she hit that tune, everyone was tapping their feet and singing along.

G-Rydah jumped in with a wicked freestyle, so Fatima just complimented it by supplying some free flow background vocals. The scene turned into a spontaneous jam session, that is, until Craig and Javon walked in.

"Yo, Craig, shorty is official!" G-Rydah exclaimed, approaching Craig as he walked in. Some of his entourage were voicing their own approval as well. Craig looked around the room. He could smell the marijuana and was obviously not pleased with what was going on.

"Good to see everyone agrees. Hopefully, we can get some work done before someone calls the cops on us," he commented sarcastically. Then, turning to G-Rydah, he said, "This is a recording studio, not a hang out. That means the drugs and liquor have to go. As a matter of fact, anyone who is not recording has to go."

A round of grumbling followed his announcement. The group was reluctant to leave.

"They're here to support me. These are my boys, they keep me motivated." G-Rydah was trying to speak up on behalf of his crew, but Craig was not in the mood.

"They have to wait outside; this is business. We have serious work to do here and we don't need the added distractions."

"But—"

"But nothing. The fun and games are over. This remix is set to push out your CD; that means it has to be perfect. Either you're ready for the big times or you're not. So what's it going to be?" Craig chided G-Rydah.

"You know I'm ready, Craig."

"Then be a professional. When you come in here, come to work. Now please ask your friends to meet you later; we have a lot of work to take care of." G-Rydah walked his crew to the door and watched them file out of the studio. Javon, who had been watching the scene, made his way over to Fatima.

"I see you manage to captivate every crowd," Javon commented.

"Well, music is my thing," Fatima answered.

"It's not hard to tell. You know, Craig is expecting great things from you; we all are."

"I'm going to do my best not to let anyone down."

"From what I've heard so far, I don't think you could even if you tried."

While the producers and techies set everything up, Fatima began to think about the strange trip that had landed her here. She had begun singing when she was five years old, dreaming and waiting for the opportunity to make it all come true in a big way.

About eight years ago, Fatima was down in Atlanta. She was fifteen years old at the time and still in high school. She sang for the school choir. Her music teacher always encouraged her to sing; she believed in Fatima. Two of her high school friends, who also sang in the choir, got together with Fatima to form a group. They called it the "Young Divas." One of the girls' mothers managed them. They would all sing at local events and talent shows. They stayed together for about two years, but the disappointment of not getting that big break caused them turmoil, and in 1997 they broke up.

Fortunately, by then, Fatima had caught the attention of Chris Baylor. He was one of the biggest stars out that year. His debut album had gone triple platinum and spawned four number one hits. Chris was even in line for a Grammy nomination. When he started his own label, he asked Fatima to sign on as his artist. She felt so lucky, she wasted no time in signing the contract.

The first meeting they had was at his estate in Buckhead. They spoke about the image he wanted for her and the possibility of her being the opening act on his tour. Fatima was excited, to say the least. When the meeting was over, he called up to the front gate and had his driver bring the car around to take her home. On the way out the door, he gave her a hug and let his hand slip down to caress her ass. He held her like that for a few seconds. Fatima wasn't sure how to react. She didn't want to offend him, so in the end, she did nothing.

All the way home, Fatima felt disgusted with herself. She

reached home and was too embarrassed to tell anyone. She just went upstairs and took a hot shower, trying to wash away the dirty feeling she had.

That night, Fatima tossed and turned, upset with herself for not having said or done anything. But by the morning, she had rationalized and convinced herself that she was overreacting. After all, she was only seventeen, while Chris was twenty-nine. She assumed she must have misread the situation. She was probably making a big deal out of nothing.

Fatima continued to go to school and work on her music. She also did background vocals with a couple of other girls on a few of Chris' songs. There was a general excitement about the upcoming tour. Talk that R. Kelly and Jodeci would be on the line-up for the tour made it clear that it was destined to be the biggest tour that year. Fatima saw all her dreams finally coming true. Then, the night of the party at Chris' house changed everything.

It was a big platinum celebration party. Chris' latest single had gone platinum in its first three weeks. Fatima had done the vocals on the track and was as excited as anyone else. Everyone showed up at the party. Chris was the new rising superstar and everyone wanted to latch on to the star. The party was filled with movie stars, athletes and even a few politicians. Fatima had never seen so many famous people in one place before. She soaked it all in, loving every minute of it. Midway through the night, Chris found Fatima talking to one of the girls from an up and coming group called Destiny's Child. He grabbed her hand excitedly and dragged her away. Fatima followed him, not sure where he was taking her.

"I got something to show you."

They reached his back room and she froze, amazed by the sight. All around the walls hung platinum and gold records.

"That's it. Go take a look." He was pointing out the latest platinum record that had been added to the collection. Fatima stared at it in awe. She wanted to reach out and touch it, but was too nervous to do so.

"Ain't it beautiful?" he beamed. It was. It was the most beautiful sight she had ever seen, and it filled her with wonder.

"You helped me get that one and soon you're going to have a room full of your own."

Fatima could barely take her eyes off it. Then she felt him behind her. He was pressing his body against hers. His erection pressed against her rear as his hands reached up to cup her breast.

"You part of the family, now, Fatima. I'm going to take care of you. You're my little chocolate girl." His breath smelled faintly of liquor.

"Chris, I don't want this," Fatima said timidly. But he ignored her and continued to fondle her young breasts, his hard-on grinding against her ass.

"Your body's so firm," he mumbled, in his own world.

"NO, CHRIS! LET ME GO!" Fatima pulled away from him. Anger flooded into his face and she was unsure what he would do next.

"What the hell is wrong with you? I'M TRYING TO LOOK OUT FOR YOU AND SHOW YOU SOME LOVE, and you're acting like your black ass too good for me?"

"Chris, it ain't like that, I just—"

"Bitch, I don't want to hear shit! Don't nobody give a fuck about what you think or want. You see all them motherfuckers out there? Huh, bitch? Who you think they're out here to see? You? Nah, bitch, they're here to see me. I'm the fucking star here. If you think for one minute that I'm doing all this work for your black ass to ride in on my coat tails for free, you got another thing coming."

"Let me tell you how this game goes," he said, pointing in her face. "I own your black ass. Right now, you're just another back up singer trying to get on. There's a million more just like you, waiting in the wings. So if you ever want to make it in this industry, you better learn to take care of those who take care of you."

Fatima stood there shocked, scared and hoping someone would come save her, but there was no savior coming. There was only Chris, holding her future in his hands. Tears began to well up in her eyes. Chris looked at her and reached out for her. Facing her, he laid his hands on her shoulders in a consoling manner.

"Listen, I'm not trying to be unreasonable, here, but you ain't no little girl; this is the way the game is played. Everyone pays their dues on one way or another." Fatima looked down, not sure what to say, not wanting to do the wrong thing, yet feeling totally powerless to even help herself. Chris took her chin in his hand, lifting her face up to look in her eyes.

"You want to sing right? You do want to be part of this tour don't you? Well, I'm going to make all that possible for you. So it's really up to you. Do you want to be part of our team? Huh?" Fatima nodded. "Good, then show me." He pressed down on her shoulders until she was kneeling in front of him, then he unzipped his pants and pulled out his dick. "Put it in your mouth and show me you're down for me," he instructed her.

Fatima thought about all the people who had sacrificed for her, thought about all the people who were counting on her. Most of all, she thought about her dreams, and she knew she didn't want to give them up, no matter what. She didn't want to go back to nothing, so she swallowed her pride, and then she swallowed him. When he was through with her, she went into the bathroom and threw up.

Chris never took her on tour, and he never worked on her CD. After that night, Fatima didn't exist to him. Eventually their record label let her CD go. Fatima had sold her dignity and her soul for an illusion.

For months, Fatima spent her nights crying herself to sleep. Then, on prom night of 1998, when all the other girls her age were dressed in their prom dresses celebrating their release from the world of high school, Fatima stayed in her room and sought her own release. On that night, she took 20 sleeping pills and said goodbye to the world. Fatima didn't die that night, not in the way she planned. But a part of her did die.

It had taken a lot for her to make the revolution back to that place where music drove her and bore witness to who she was. In a way, Chris was right—everybody pays their dues in one way or another. Fatima nearly paid with her life, but she learned an important lesson along the way. If you don't believe in yourself, no one else will.

"Fatima!" They were calling her back into the booth. She went in and blew like never before.

Two hours later, they had finished two versions of the single. G-Rydah rapping and Fatima singing the hooks and background. Everyone in the room felt it in their bones, they had just produced a classic.

FIFTEEN | Peaches arrived at Nana's house. Nana lived

in Freeport, Long Island. It had once been one of the better neighborhoods, but crime and drugs had crept in over time. It was still a decent enough place when compared to most of the city. She lived in a nice-sized private home with Tiffany.

Peaches parked the car, pulled the packages out from the back seat and made her way to the front door. When she rang the bell, Nana opened the door.

"Peaches! Come in, baby. It's good to see you!" Nana always made Peaches feel welcomed in her house.

"It's good to see you, too, Nana." Peaches walked in, dropped the packages and gave Nana a big hug.

"Tiffany's over at a friend's house, she should be coming along soon. I hope you ain't buying that girl more stuff," she commented, glaring at the many packages sitting on the floor.

"Nana, its just a few things for the summer."

"You're spoiling that girl. She's already got more stuff than she knows what to do with."

"I want her to look good, Nana."

"The girl is only thirteen years old. You shouldn't be putting thoughts of looking good in her head at that age," Nana chided.

"I know, Nana, I know, don't worry. I'll take it easy."

"Okay, now come in here and give me a hand fixing dinner."

Nana was seventy years old and still got around with as much vigor as women half her age. She was actually Peaches' grandmother, and she had raised her from the time Peaches was fifteen. That's how old she was when she got pregnant, and Suzy Q kicked her out.

After the incident with Bobby on the staircase, Peaches could see the look of desire in his eyes whenever he came to the house. One day, when Troy was having a hookie party, Peaches heard Troy take his girlfriend upstairs to his room. She knew he would be there for some time, so she snuck downstairs and made her way to the kitchen looking for Bobby. When Bobby saw her, he came into the kitchen.

"What you doing down here?" he asked.

"I live here, I can go where I want," Peaches replied sarcastically.

"You know Troy don't want you down here when we around."

Though he was talking like he was trying to scold her, Peaches could still see that same look of desire in his eyes.

"Did you like the way my butt felt?"

The question caught him off guard. He didn't answer.

"You want to feel it again, don't you?" Peaches continued to tease him.

Bobby was feeling uncomfortable. Peaches moved closer to him and he stepped back, unsure if he should respond.

"I'm going upstairs to my room; you can come up if you want."

Walking away, Peaches didn't even look back; she knew he was watching her. She added a little sway to her hips to excite him, then she made her way up to her room and left the door open. Not even ten minutes later, Bobby was at her door. Peaches let him in, then locked the door behind him. Now that he was actually there, Peaches became a little nervous, but she wanted so badly to experience what she saw in his eyes that she wasn't going to turn him back now.

Peaches came to him, embracing him, her body against his.

Immediately, she could feel his body wanting hers. He touched her and her body was engulfed in flames. The feeling Peaches was experiencing from the way he explored her body excited her. She watched almost detached as he peeled her clothes off and laid her down on the bed.

Then, Bobby began to play inside her private places with his fingers. Though she had touched herself there before, his touch was different. It bothered her at first, but soon, she found her body moving with the rhythm of his fingers. As he continued to manipulate her, the strangeness of his touch began to feel good to her. She lifted her hips to meet his hands.

Somewhere in her mind, thoughts were gathering like a voice she could barely hear. Still, she understood it. The voice was saying, *You're only thirteen years old.* Although Peaches felt that fact should have made her feel ashamed of what she was doing, it didn't. All she kept thinking was, *I'm only thirteen but he's here with me, instead of the girls his own age downstairs. He knows Troy will kill him if he finds out, but he's here anyway.* In spite of all the reasons he shouldn't have been there, he was, and knowing he wanted her that bad made Peaches feel warm all over, but especially between her legs.

Peaches let out a soft moan. She was feeling so good, but he stopped. She didn't want him to stop. She was about to tell him it wasn't a bad moan, but he reached for her, pulling her to him then he turned her around. He positioned her on all fours and then entered her from behind. Peaches felt him open her up. It wasn't his finger anymore, and it hurt a little. Still, when he moved, she moved with him and the more he moved the better it felt. He grabbed her ass, squeezing it in his grip, thrusting harder and faster, in and out of her. It didn't last long; in about a minute he was done. That was her first time, the beginning.

Three months later, Troy went to prison, sentenced 25 years to life. Bobby no longer worried that Troy would catch him, and started coming around more often. He wasn't the only one.

Other boys would stop by, also. Peaches learned to get what she wanted in exchange for what they wanted; after all, ain't nothing in this life free.

"Mommy!" Peaches heard Tiffany yelling as she came through the door.

"I'm in the kitchen with Nana!" she shouted back. Tiffany came running in and gave Peaches a big hug. This was her pride and joy.

"How's my baby?" she asked.

"Mommy, I'm not a baby anymore," Tiffany answered with mock annoyance.

Peaches knew it was true. She was getting bigger everyday, and her body was far more matured than her age. Peaches worried sometimes, but not that much. She knew Tiffany was in good hands with Nana.

"Well, excuse me, Ms. I ain't a baby anymore."

"Mommy, you spending the night?" Tiffany asked.

"Maybe, if it's all right with Nana." Peaches turned to look at Nana.

"Child, please, you've always been welcome here," Nana proclaimed.

"Good!" exclaimed Tiffany, settling the matter. "What did you buy me?"

"Well, let me wash my hands and we'll take a look."

Peaches washed her hands, dried them off on a small dish rag and went into the front room. She took one bag with some Baby Phat shirts and passed it to Tiffany.

"These are nice, Mommy." She was pleased.

"I got you some Rocawear for girls, too."

Peaches had bought her jeans, sneakers, boots, sweat suits, games for her Xbox, CDs and DVDs. When Nana walked into the room, her face frowned up at all the stuff laid out across the room, but she didn't say anything to ruin Tiffany's moment.

Peaches loved buying her things. She wanted Tiffany to have everything she desired; everything Peaches didn't have when she was her age. Most of all, she wanted her to know that her mommy would always be there for her, no matter what. Not like Suzy Q.

By the time Peaches was 15 years old, she had a reputation. It didn't bother her. Though it was true that she would give it up, just anyone wasn't getting into her panties. She was in Jamaica High School then, and her main boyfriend (because she had a few), was a guy named Supreme. He was 19, and had dropped out of high school years before to hustle. He kept Peaches looking good and her pockets right. She would have to sneak him in the house when he came to visit, because Suzy Q didn't like him.

By this time, Suzy Q also had a main man. His name was JT. He was 32, which made him five years younger than Suzy Q. JT was infamous; a sort of neighborhood legend, as far as bad boys were concerned. He grew up in the South Side and terrorized it since his teens. He'd recently come home from prison six months earlier. He had done eight years for shooting a drug dealer who refused to pay for the privilege of selling on the block, and people still feared JT. He had had a thing for Suzy Q before he left for prison; now that he was back, he saw the opportunity and made his move. Suzy Q was flattered that JT was still attracted to her, not to mention that he was a man well respected around the neighborhood. She gave into his attention and one thing lead to another. Now, he was a regular around the house as well.

One day, when Peaches knew Suzy Q was upstairs asleep, she snuck Supreme into the house. Supreme wanted to go to a hotel, but Peaches, thinking that hotel money would be better spent buying her some new earrings, convinced him that Suzy Q would be asleep and they had nothing to worry about. As luck would have it, Suzy Q was asleep, and it didn't take long for Supreme to have Peaches kneeling in front of the sofa, face in the cushion, bent over, getting fucked doggy style. With every thrust, Peaches felt him slapping against her ass.

Then, suddenly, he was thrown backwards, hitting the floor hard. Peaches turned to find Supreme on his back, his pants around his ankles, and JT standing over him with a gun in Supreme's face.

"Don't shoot him!" Peaches cried out.

"Why not? I thought your mother told this boy not to be in her house."

Supreme lay motionless, fear clearly written on his face. He knew who JT was and had no doubt that the slightest wrong move would end up with him being shot.

"It's my fault, JT, I brought him in here," Peaches pleaded.

"Yeah, but the boy knows better." JT cocked the hammer.

"Please, please, don't shoot him. I swear I won't do it again." Peaches could see that JT was considering the circumstances, probably wondering if he could get away with shooting the boy in the house.

"Okay, boy, get your pants on and get the fuck out of here before I change my mind." JT released the hammer and Supreme got up half dressed and made his way to the door without uttering a word. Peaches was left standing there naked and embarrassed, but most of all, scared about JT telling her mother.

"You going to tell Suzy Q?" Peaches asked.

JT looked at her. "Put your clothes on, and yeah, I'm telling her." Peaches turned to grab her T-shirt. Her jeans and panties were on the other side of the room. She pulled her T-Shirt on but didn't move from the spot to get the rest of her clothes. She was too afraid that JT would walk right upstairs and tell Suzy Q what had happened. Since she was positioned between him and the stairs, she was the only thing preventing him from getting to her mother.

"JT, I know I was wrong, but if you tell Suzy Q, she'll throw me out, you know how she is," Peaches tried to reason with him.

"Yeah, and you know how she is, too, which is why you should have thought of that before you brought that boy up here."

JT tried to walk past her, but she blocked his path. He tried to push her to the side, but she grabbed him, wrapping her arms around him.

"Girl, what the hell is wrong with you? Get the fuck off me."

"Please, JT, don't tell Suzy Q; I swear it won't ever happen again."

She was desperate to stop him, trying to hold him back, and that's when nature took over. Peaches was a young woman with a firm, thick, halfway naked body pressed against a man who had only been home from prison a few months. JT's body responded like most any man's would. She felt him hardening against her as they struggled. Then she realized what she had to do. Before he knew what she was doing, Peaches jerked the pants of his Fila sweat suit down, exposing the erection straining at his boxers.

"If you do me a favor, I'll do you a favor."

She looked him in the eyes to let him know how serious she was. He looked at her, but said nothing, so she pulled him out the front of his boxers, and though at first sight she was a little surprised by how much more bigger than Supreme he was, she took him in her mouth and began to lick and suck him like never before. He let out a soft moan and grabbed a handful of hair. That let Peaches know he was hers, so she gave him the pleasure he wanted.

When he was ready to explode she pulled her mouth off him, and kneeled in front of the sofa, bent over, with her ass in the air. In a few seconds, she felt his hands gripping her hips. He positioned himself behind her and then slid into her. JT was a lot larger than Supreme, and that thrilled Peaches. Now she knew what a real man felt like, and she began smiling as JT pumped away inside her.

For months after that, Peaches and Suzy Q shared the same

man, although only Peaches knew it. JT became her secret obsession. He wasn't like any of the boys she had before. He turned her out in ways she would never have dreamed possible. He introduced her to the oral pleasures a man could give a woman. The first time he went down on her, she cried because it felt so good. JT gave her her first orgasm, and he also introduced her to her first anal experience. The way he fucked her every time they were together made her fiend for him when they were apart. Before long, she knew she was in love with him, but he was Suzy Q's man. Peaches dreamed of him leaving Suzy Q and taking her away from there.

Whenever JT and Suzy Q had an argument, she silently prayed this would be the day he would leave her. Instead, JT would leave the house upset and come back late, when he knew Suzy Q would be asleep. On those nights he would stay downstairs, most of the time sitting in the dark. In her heart, Peaches always knew he was waiting for her. Although he never called her, she knew it anyway, and she would come to his side. Those were the times he fucked her rough and hard. He punished her for what he wanted to do to Suzy Q. Peaches understood his anger; Suzy Q was always making someone angry. So she gave him her body to console him. As he penetrated her deeply and pounded out his frustrations on her, she was proud to give him what she knew Suzy Q wasn't.

After five months, Peaches was pregnant. She was happy for them, but when she told JT the news, he wanted no part of it. He told her to get an abortion, but she refused. She knew sooner or later he would think about it and realize they were meant to be together. He never did. Eventually, he left. He left Suzy Q, left Peaches and left his daughter before she was even born. When Peaches told Suzy Q she was pregnant, she threw her out. It was Nana who took her in and Nana who helped Peaches raise her baby, Tiffany.

Peaches learned never to give her heart to any man again. Her precious Tiffany became the joy of her life, and Peaches had given her everything. She made sure Tiffany would not want for anything simply because her father had abandoned her. She refused to be one of those mothers on welfare, waiting for some man to take care of her and her child, so, she started dancing in the clubs to make sure her baby was taken care of.

"I have one more thing for you, baby."

"What is it, Mommy?" Tiffany's eyes were wide with expectation.

"First, give Mommy some love." Tiffany jumped up, coming over to give Peaches a big hug, which made her feel great.

"You know I love you, right, baby?" Peaches whispered in her ear.

"Yeah, Mommy, I know, and I love you too."

"I got you a chain and pendant so you wouldn't forget." She gave Tiffany the chain. It was gold and had a gold pendant with diamonds that read "MOMMY'S LITTLE GIRL."

Tiffany looked at it, then gave Peaches another big hug. "Thank you, Mommy, I love it." Tiffany meant everything to Peaches.

"Okay, now, let's put this stuff up and get ready for dinner," Nana said, putting an end to all the gift giving.

Tiffany got up and started gathering her things. She was a good girl and Peaches was proud of her. She knew Nana was doing a good job raising her.

"Peaches, come help me set the table." Nana walked toward the kitchen and Peaches followed her. "How are things with you, baby?"

"I'm okay, Nana."

"Listen to me; I know you love that child, but those presents don't make up for her mama. She needs to see you more, " Nana scolded.

"Nana, I try to make it out here as much as possible."

"Which is once a week. If you want that girl to know you as more than some weekly stranger bearing gifts, you got to spend more time with her."

"How am I supposed to do that?"

"You can let the child move in with you."

"Nana, you know I can't do that, I work at night. How am I supposed to leave her in the house all night by herself?"

"You ever thought about getting a real job?" She gave Peaches a stern look.

"Nana, please, let's not argue about that now," Peaches pleaded.

"We are not arguing, but honey, you need to think about your future. You're 28 years old. How much longer you think you going to be able to do that kind of work?"

"Okay, Nana, you're right, and I'm going to work something out; just give me some time to figure things out."

"You know this house is big enough for both y'all; you can always move back in and spend time with Tiffany, but you got to get yourself a real job. But I can't have you living here and working in those clubs."

"I'll think about it, Nana. I promise."

Peaches didn't want to give up her place or her job, but she wasn't in the mood to argue with Nana.

Tiffany came running into the dining room. They sat down, had a family dinner, then later, they all sat around eating ice cream and watching television. Although in her heart Peaches knew that staying there would be a good thing for Tiffany and herself, she just wasn't ready to give up dancing, yet.

Peaches spent that night at Nana's house, then left the next morning, leaving an envelope with $1,000 on the table. Tiffany was in good hands with Nana, and that's all that mattered.

SIXTEEN | After they had finished recording in the studio, Fatima was starving. She hadn't eaten all day. G-Rydah left quickly, in a hurry to catch up with his boys. Javon invited Craig and Fatima out to eat, but Craig declined, stating he had already promised his wife he'd be home for dinner. So, Fatima and Javon went out by themselves.

Fatima didn't have a car; she always joked that her middle name was public transportation, so when she jumped in Javon's six series Benz, she was impressed. When he threw in the Dead Prez CD she was surprised. He looked about two or three years older, but his demeanor was of someone much older, so a Hip Hop CD, and especially a Dead Prez CD, seemed out of place for him.

Fatima did notice how extremely good looking he was, yet his most impressive facet was his mannerisms. The way he carried himself, you could tell he was a man used to being in charge. It was easy to imagine that he and Craig were close, and for some reason, Fatima really felt good about her future in their hands.

Fatima and Javon reached the 40/40 club in Manhattan, got a table and ordered their food.

"You were great today," Javon complimented her.

"Thank you, Mr. Williams."

"Please, call me Javon. Mr. Williams sounds like an old man."

"Okay, Javon it is. That's a unique name; I've never heard of anyone else with it."

"Yeah, well, my father named me, and from what I hear, he

was a pretty unique individual himself," Javon explained.

"You didn't know him?"

"He died before I had the opportunity."

"I'm sorry to hear that."

"Thank you. What about you, though? With a name like Fatima Amir, I take it you're a Muslim?"

"Actually, I was born into the religion. My mother and father were both Islamic, but I haven't really practiced the religion since being in America."

"You're not American?" he asked, surprised.

"No, I was born in Africa."

"Oh, yeah, so you're a real African Princess, huh?"

"At your service." Fatima smiled and bowed her head.

"Does your family live here now?"

"No, Mama died years ago, and Baba, that's what I call my father, still lives in Africa."

"I'm sorry to hear about your mother."

"Death happens a lot in my country."

"It happens a lot here, too."

The way he said it, Fatima knew he was speaking from experience.

Her mind drifted to the woman she had known for far too short a period of time. Mama was born on the island of Zanzibar. Her name was Salamah, and she was a beautiful dark-skinned African woman. She worked as a school teacher in Tanzania and had a spirit that made everyone who met her trust and respect her.

Most amazing was her voice. Mama could sing, really sing. Fatima's fondest memories of her were those times Mama would sing to her. In African culture, music is a form of expression used to communicate and share life's lessons with the people. Mama, who taught many of the community's children in the government school, would use song to teach tribal histories in ways that school books couldn't. She was seen as a woman upon whom the creator had bestowed a special gift, and as a little girl, Fatima felt blessed to live in the same house as Mama.

As far back as Fatima could remember, from the moment she first learned to carry a tune, she would join Mama as she sang and worked around the house. Life wasn't easy, it never is, but with Mama and Baba, Fatima was in a safe and secure place. That's what's most important when you're a little child, that feeling of comfort and security. Yet, it wasn't too much later that Mama's death shattered that feeling. Baba and Fatima learned the hard way that life offers no securities. Fate is a thief in the night; it can come and take away a loved one at anytime it chooses. When Fatima was ten years old, Mama died of AIDS.

AIDS is a major problem all over Africa. Most of the country doesn't have the facilities, technology or knowledge to deal with the epidemic, so millions of Africans die each year.

Mama's death was so devastating, it was felt by all in the township, but it took its hardest toll on her family, for Mama was indeed the spirit that breathed life into both Baba and Fatima. Fatima remembered the feeling of powerlessness as she watched Mama die slowly before her. Baba, who had been a warrior all his life, was hurt the most. He watched his wife's life being stripped away by a disease he could do little about. Looking back now, Fatima thought that event more than anything else influenced him to send her to America.

Baba disapproved of America's politics, but he knew the country's economic wealth offered the best opportunity and quality of living for a child. Yeah, Baba was a warrior, but he was also a father, so he sent Fatima to live with his family in America. It wasn't easy for Fatima in the States, but her music helped her heal the hurt that was deep down in her soul. Although she sometimes felt like a motherless child, most times, when she sang, Fatima could feel Mama harmonizing right along with her.

"Where did Craig find you?" The question brought her back

to the present.

"He didn't, I found him."

"Yeah?"

"Yeah, I saw what Keynote Management was doing for G-Rydah, and I thought if I had that type of push behind me, I could make it in this industry. So I went to him and the rest, as they say, is history."

"That was a smart move. Craig is good at what he does."

"I know, I did my homework."

"You don't leave much to chance, do you?"

"Let's just say, I've seen the ugly side of this business before. So I'm a lot more careful now."

"I can understand that, but like my old man use to say, 'Sometimes you got to go through hell to come out right'."

"Well, I've been through my share of hell; I'm ready for things to get right!"

"I know what you mean."

They talked, laughed and shared their thoughts more comfortably than either would have thought possible, for people who were basically strangers. Fatima found Javon interesting, but even more than that, they shared a connection. From the outside, he looked like a man who had it all, but she sensed he wasn't happy. Almost like he was still searching for answers to questions he didn't even know. In a way, she thought that was part of their connection. They were both far from where they wanted to be, where they had to be, if they were truly going to be happy. Though in her case, she knew the path that would lead her to happiness and she was marching down that road now. As

for Javon, she believed he hadn't found his way, yet.

That was the sad part—everybody has that one thing which makes them complete, that one thing which becomes the source of their happiness. Some people knew early in life what their "thing" was; for Fatima it was music. Music was her purpose, the thing she was born to do, the reason she existed. Others never figured it out, and those were the ones that went through life never really happy. If that was Javon, then Fatima felt sorry for him.

After they ate, he dropped her off at home. Before leaving, she invited him to stop by the community center where she worked. She didn't even know why. No, that's a lie. The truth was, for the first time in a long time, Fatima had enjoyed herself, and she was looking forward to more of Javon's company. She just had to pray it didn't come with all the drama.

Triple Crown Publications presents . . .

SEVENTEEN | Javon and Derrick were cruising down
Fulton Street, headed to the club. This wasn't a party spot, it was
a private social club. Members-only type of thing. All the mem-
bers were a part of the crew in one way or another. Even the girls
who came in there were either bag up girls or mules. It was a spot
for the hustlers to relax and discuss business, away from nosy out-
siders.

Inside the club, there was a bar, pool tables, some video games,
a large screen TV with cable hook up, and a few tables spotted
around the room. The back room was usually where the gambling
took place. Sometimes, big games went down with as much as ten
or twenty thousand hanging on the roll of a dice. People were only
searched on special occasions, so most of the time, there were
enough guns in the place to start a small war. In the year since the
club had been open, there had been only one person shot, so no
one saw any reason to raise the level of security.

The one rule the club did have was no drugs. Personal use was
okay. You could smoke, drink, or sniff, but no direct transactions
or carrying large quantities of drugs into the club. Of course drug
deals went down regularly in the club, but only the negotiations
took place inside; the actual transactions were held elsewhere.

Derrick pulled his navigator up in front of the club and double parked. They got out and made their way inside. Javon quickly surveyed the environment, found the empty table toward the
rear, elbowed Derrick and they began making their way to it. After

taking off his jacket and draping it across the back of his chair, Javon headed over to the bar to get two beers. When he returned, Black Justice and Shelly were at the table.

"Look, we got to push this thing tomorrow," Black Justice was emphasizing to Derrick.

"I can't go tomorrow," Shelly complained.

Shelly was one of the crew's most trusted mules. She was a pro at carrying product, cash, guns–you name it, if it had to go across the state line, Shelly was the best one for the job. Black Justice was the man out in B-more. He had been with them about three or four years. Two years ago, some stick-up kids tried to rob him, unfortunately for them. Black Justice never went anywhere without his gun. As he often joked, it was his American Express card; he never left home without it. A minute into the robbery, Black was trotting away, leaving two bodies on the pavement in front of his girlfriend's house.

Derrick got him together and slid him over to Baltimore to lay low. Over the last year he had put together a little team out there and was copping his weight from Javon and Derrick. Tonight, he wanted to cop two bricks and have Shelly transport it to Baltimore tomorrow.

"I told my man I was going to visit him tomorrow," Shelly said.

"What's up?" Javon inquired, taking his seat.

"Jay, I got to get some shit back to B-more, yo, by tomorrow."

"So, what's the problem?"

"Shelly's talking about going up north to see some nigga in prison tomorrow."

"Not some nigga, my nigga!" Shelly corrected him.

"Shelly, can't you see him when you get back?"

"Nah, Jay, they having one of those prison festivals tomorrow, and I already promised him I was coming. I can't miss it."

"Black, why don't you get someone else?"

"Where am I going to get someone this late in the game? Jay, she's the only one who knows the trip well enough to make the move on short notice."

Javon could see Black's point, but he didn't want to pressure Shelly into doing something she didn't want to do.

"Look, Black, if I was you, I'd either start looking for someone else or start making arrangements to take it yourself," Derrick spoke up.

"What? We talking about business here. What's more important?" Black Justice was upset that Derrick had taken Shelly's side.

"Depends on who you ask," Derrick responded.

"You, Jay ..." He turned to Javon, but he just shrugged, indicating he wanted nothing to do with it.

"Black, we get the bricks for you, tell us where you want to meet tomorrow, and we'll get it to you, but you're gonna have to take it from there," Derrick stated in between sips of beer.

"Yeah, all right, let me make some calls. We'll set it up for later on tonight," Black stated, pulling out his cell phone and walking away.

"Thanks, Derrick," Shelly said.

"Don't sweat it. What's up with homie? When is he coming home?"

"He sees his second board in another year. They might cut him loose."

"You taking him something up?"

"Nah, I don't want him fucking with that. He's too close to the door to be playing them type of games."

"I feel you." Derrick reached into his pocket, pulled out a knot, peeled off five one hundred dollar bills and pressed them into Shelly's hand. "Here, for his commissary."

"Thanks, Derrick." Shelly bent down and kissed him on the cheek, then left.

Javon took a sip of his beer, thought about the situation a little, then decided to ask, "Why did you take her side? Her man ain't even down with us. "

"Loyalty."

"Loyalty?"

"Yeah, she was showing loyalty to her man and you should always reward loyalty. Besides, Black is a veteran; he's supposed to have a back-up plan."

"Okay, I agree with the part about Black, but you and I both know that Shelly is out here fucking other cats, and that ain't no loyalty."

Derrick sipped his beer, put the bottle down on the table, then looked Javon straight in the eyes and said, "Jay, you're confusing loyalty with faithfulness."

"That's semantics."

"No, it's not. It's reality. Her man is up north; if he thinks she's not out here fucking, then he's either a fool or a square, 'cause those are the only types of niggas who expect a woman to stay faithful. The important thing is, she's taking care of her responsibility as his woman and that's the real definition of loyalty."

"So, you telling me if you was Upstate and your girl was out here fucking, you'd be all right with that?"

"As long as she was taking care of her responsibilities toward me, I'd have to accept that."

"Nah, homie, I didn't say accept that. Would you be *all right* with it?"

"Jay, I'm not saying I would like it, but yeah, I'd be all right with it ... think about this—if your girl was in prison for ten years would you be out here fucking?"

"That's different."

"Why, 'cause you're a man? You think a woman don't have the same needs? Jay, nobody would blame you if you were out here fucking, but if you just left her and didn't hold her down, people would look at you like a piece of shit and they'd be right. Shelly visits her man every month. She sends him money, packages and helped pay for his lawyer. So what if she's out here fucking, she handled her responsibilities; that's what's important."

"Yeah, I guess." Javon could see Derrick's point. He had never been in prison, but he knew plenty of homies whose women did nothing for them while they were down. He couldn't even count how many phone calls he got from Upstate asking him to step to some girl 'cause she wasn't on her job. They never called and said stop her from fucking, so it looked like Derrick had a legitimate point. Javon's thoughts drifted and he found himself wondering about Fatima. Earlier, he'd stopped by the community center to see her. They'd had such a good time talking the night before, so when she invited him, he was curious enough about her to take her up on the offer.

The center was in the Bedford Stuyvesant section of Brooklyn. It really wasn't more than a converted storefront, but you could tell efforts were made to make it comfortable for the children. Fatima and two others ran the place. There were about fifteen children at the center, spanning in age range from about seven to fourteen. Fatima took time out to show him around, and even introduced him to some of the kids. They were busy working on a black history project.

Javon looked around. He noticed all the pictures of black leaders and the red, black and green flags that hung on the walls. He was pretty knowledgeable about black history. He had learned a lot from Raheem when he was young, and then again, when he was in college. Javon knew that at one time, black people had the most civilized culture in the world, but it was sure hard to tell by looking around now.

He had learned a lot by reading the often suggested books of Chancellor Williams, Dr. Henrick Clarke, Ivan Van Sertima and Naim Akbar, but in the end, when he needed money for his mother's hospital bills, all the information didn't mean anything. He learned the greatest lesson about black people; namely that black life wasn't worth much unless you happened to also be blessed with money. In the end, money was what counted.

Plenty of people, both black and white, were willing to sit back and let his mother die if he couldn't pay for her treatment. In a way, he respected people like Fatima and her friends. They were trying to rebuild black people; he just wasn't sure it was possible. He had looked at those little kids at the center, knowing half of them would be in a prison or a grave by the time they were twenty-five. It was a hard reality, but reality nonetheless.

"Javon, these cats down in Miami got some good product and we getting it at a decent price."

Derrick's words brought Javon back to the here and now.

"Yeah, it's working out good," Javon responded.

"Right now, we pushing six kilos a week. With E-Money down in North Carolina, and Black Jack pushing up for more, we could get up to seven or eight kilos a week."

"Yeah, that sounds good." Javon sipped his beer.

"Not to mention that with Manny out of the way, the rest of them cats in East New York are small time. If we put enough product on the streets, we'll shut them down in no time."

"You think that's smart?" Javon wasn't liking the way this conversation was going.

"We can ease it in or push it through someone who's already out there. The point is, right now we're pushing six a week but if we make the right moves, we can be up to ten, maybe twelve a week in about a month."

"That means we have to cop more than we're getting now."

Derrick was definitely on a roll now. Javon could read the excitement in his eyes.

"Yeah, that's exactly what I was thinking. Check it, we got to make a move down to Miami this week coming. I say, let's stop by North Carolina first and get a feel for what E-Money is going to need, then go see the connect in Miami and discuss making a big move at the end of the month. "

"How big?"

"Fifty kilos."

"Fifty kilos?!"

"Yeah, let's say we negotiate seven and a half a brick, half up front and half on consignment. That's about twice what we're paying now for ten on the front half; the back half we don't have to worry about. We'll see that in the first few bricks we flip; everything else is us."

"How do we know they got that? Or that they'll give it to us for that price?"

"That's what we need to find out when we get down there. Jay, we got the money and the time is right. This is where we take it to the next level; it's either now or never."

"Yeah, now or never," Javon repeated.

Triple Crown Publications presents . . .

EIGHTEEN | Javon and Derrick arrived in North Carolina early in the morning. They called E-Money to let him know they were in town, then drove to the safe house he had set up. They had figured on staying about two days in North Carolina to get a vibe on how E-Money had things flowing. Then, they'd ride down to Miami and meet with the connect.

They were carrying about $100,000 in cash. They knew that driving a non-descript car and staying low was absolutely necessary since they didn't want to draw any unwarranted attention. You can believe, there is no way two twenty-something-year-old black men can explain $100,000 to the satisfaction of a nosy sheriff. To tell the truth it wouldn't matter if they could; in this game, the key to success is knowing how to be invisible.

When they reached the safe house, E-Money was there with three of his boys: Black, Money and Breeze. E-Money schooled them on the operation. The safe house was in a quiet area that didn't attract much attention. He had another apartment he shared with a local girl out in the hood he hustled in. Anyone who has ever hustled out of town knows the mechanics of the game. OT hustling is grounded on finding a way into the hood. Ninety percent of the time, it's through a local girl.

Certain things were automatic. For example, New York hustlers were hated everywhere they went, though not by the women. Women out of town loved New York niggas, and niggas from New York loved them back. The one thing you could always count on was once someone got a foot in the door, others would surely come. Any time there's a new market to sell your product, competition comes right on your heels. That's why it's so important to establish yourself firmly so that anyone who comes afterward is forced to deal with you.

E-Money had done just that. Not only did he have product out there on the streets, but he was already selling weight to the locals. It was only ounces, but that was a good start. Today, E-Money was supposed to meet a customer that had been looking for some weight. They were meeting at the mall, so Derrick and Javon decided to tag along and watch E-Money operate. As soon as they saw the guy, they knew it was trouble.

"You see who he's meeting?" Derrick recognized him first.

"Yeah, I thought he was in the Feds."

"He was, but he cut a deal—sold out his connect and his team."

E-Money was meeting Johnny Junior, or JJ, as he was called. JJ was a big-time hustler out of Queens. He was seeing top dollar in the dope game until the Feds caught up with him. He was looking at natural life, so he took the easy way out and cut a deal.

"You think he's still working for the Feds?" Javon asked.

"He could be, or, he could be trying to get back on. You know he took down a lot of good people in New York when he snitched. It makes sense for him to come down here if he's trying to get back in the game 'cause he's too well known up top," Derrick explained. Whatever his intentions were, neither Javon nor Derrick liked the fact that he found his way to their doorstep.

"Damn, if he's working for the Feds, that means they're watching E-Money, and they're probably watching us, now." Javon took a furtive look around. An uneasy feeling was creeping up on him. "Derrick, we got to shut down."

"Nah, think about it, Jay, even if they've been watching E-Money, we just got here yesterday. We're driving a car that ain't in either one of our names, so they can't know who we are...but we do need to know what the deal is before we make any moves. "

"Okay, what's the plan?"

"If they're watching us now, they probably figure we're all going to move together. So, the first thing is to separate. They're probably not ready to follow us if we all go in different directions. Here's what we'll do: you wait 'till E-Money is done talking with JJ and let him know what time it is. Leave the cash with him and go to Miami, contact the connect, let him know that we'll be there, but let him know there will be a delay, just a day or two. Make sure you tell E-Money to stop selling. He can tell the customers he is waiting for another shipment; he'll be able to take care of them in a day or two."

"What about you?"

"I'm going to get lost in this crowd. Then, I'll meet you in a few days in Miami. In the meantime, I'll find out what I can."

Javon followed Derrick's directions. He trusted Derrick's judgment without question. Derrick had the military experience and knew the streets. At times like this, Derrick was in his element. To Javon, it was a bad omen, even if it wasn't the Feds. Close calls were usually warnings that trouble was right around the corner.

For years, they had been extremely careful, and extremely lucky. But luck was fickle and no matter how careful you were, you never knew when someone would fold and turn you in to save their own ass. That was the major reason Javon was determined to leave the game behind. A lot of players found themselves growing old and forgotten in some prison cell, simply because they didn't know when to walk away.

Derrick called two days later. He told Javon to set up a meeting with the connect. He'd be in town with the money that day.

After they had gone their separate ways, Derrick followed JJ back to his place. At three in the morning, Derrick woke JJ up by smashing the butt of a 357 in his face. The first blow broke his nose and his cheek bone and got his attention. Derrick proceeded to tie him up, then questioned him in between further blows and broken bones. JJ denied working for the Feds. Derrick carefully searched the house, then, taking his cell phone and two-way, he left JJ behind, tied up with two bullet holes in his chest and his tongue cut out. It was gruesome, but there was nothing worse in the game than a snitch. The message sent would be clearly received by those with thoughts of going that route. Derrick showed up in Miami the next day with the $100,000.

"You set the meet?" Derrick asked.

"Yeah, tomorrow. What did you learn about JJ?"

"I don't think he was working with the Feds down here."

"You don't think, but you're not sure!"

"Not yet; I told E-Money to lay low for a couple of weeks, to give me time to make a final check."

"What kind of check?"

"I got his cell phone and pager. I'm going to take them to Eddie, since he's an expert with all that computer technology. He'll pull the numbers off the memory, and then we can have Sheila over at the phone company see who he's been talking to. If no Fed number shows up, we're probably clear."

"How did you get hold of his phone and two-way?"

"Let's just say that he won't be needing them anymore," Derrick replied.

"We're going to have to be more careful."

"Jay, there's no way we could have seen this coming. It's just lucky we showed up when we did."

"Yeah, and that's what I'm worried about. How fucked up have things gotten when we have to rely on luck to get us by? Luck is a hell of a thing to gamble our lives on."

"Yeah," Derrick agreed. "Can't argue that." What Javon said made a lot of sense to Derrick, and for the first time since he had to deal with his family being in prison did he think about luck sometimes being fucked up. Yet, he loved the streets and the only thing he hated was the fatal lessons he had to teach.

NINETEEN | When Javon opened the door, he was

wearing a bathrobe. Peaches could tell he had just stepped out of the shower. She went straight into his arms, opened the front of his robe and wrapped her body inside it. She held him tightly, his slightly damp skin wet against hers. Javon had no clothes on underneath the robe. The smell of his freshly washed body excited her. Damn if it didn't make her horny.

"You missed me that much?" Javon asked with a smile. His trip down south had taken nearly a week. He was glad to be back in New York. The whole situation with JJ had rattled his nerves.

"Yeah," Peaches replied, grabbing his butt. "I missed you."

"Okay, okay, let me close the door before the neighbors call the cops on us," Javon said with a chuckle, as he led her away from the door.

"You took a shower for me?"

"I took a shower for me."

"Well, okay, let me lotion you up."

Peaches grabbed his hand and led him to the bedroom. She took off her jacket, letting it drop to the floor.

"Take your robe off and wait right here," she instructed him. She rushed to the bathroom to get a large towel and a bottle of baby oil. When she returned, Javon was standing there naked, looking good as hell. She stopped for a second to look him over.

That smile of his had a way of warming her heart. Yet, the best part was the body below the waist. As Peaches had grown fond of saying, "The boy could have been a porno star." Javon had been blessed with a good ten inches and knew exactly what to do with it, too.

"Are you just going to stand there looking at me?" Javon asked.

"Yeah, why? You shy or something?"

"Nah, I ain't shy, but don't you get paid when people look at you?"

"Oh, that's how it is, huh?" Peaches crossed her arms over her chest. "Well, just don't stand there, big boy. I shake my thing, so let me see you move something," Peaches teased him.

"All you gotta do is ask, baby." Javon began to do his impression of a strip club dance.

It looked pretty silly but Peaches thought he looked so cute that she wanted to go over to him and jump on his ass at that moment .

"You so silly," she said between giggles. "Come here." Javon went over, took her in his arms and kissed her deep, all the while, squeezing her ass. He had a way of squeezing and lifting her cheeks that opened her up and made her want to cum on herself. As he did it now, she felt like dropping the towel, the oil, her jeans and panties and climbing on this nigga immediately, but he pulled away from her.

"I've been missing you, too." He said it with such sincerity that it touched her heart. Yeah, Peaches decided he was definitely going to get her best today.

"Come on." She laid the towel on the bed. "Lay down on your stomach." Javon did as she asked. Peaches kicked off her sneakers, stepped out of her jeans, took off her sweatshirt and bra, then said fuck it, and took off her panties as well. They would play this game completely naked. Peaches climbed on Javon, straddling his lower back. She poured some oil on his back and began to massage it into his neck, shoulders and upper back. She leaned forward and licked his ear.

"Don't say anything," she instructed him, "I just want you to listen and imagine."

Javon nodded in agreement and Peaches began describing what she would do to him. "I'm going to start at your ankles and lick a warm trail up and over your tight yet ever so soft ass. Then I'll take my tongue and play in between ass cheeks while making my way around to kiss the tip of your dick." Peaches could hear Javon moan. "I said don't make a sound." Her massaging became even more aggressive than before. Javon was doing his best to not nut on the spot.

"After I kiss the tip of your dick," she continued, rubbing oil into his back and then onto his arms. "I'ma make it disappear while taking you into my mouth. And before you know it we'll have a 69 with my hot and dripping wet pink pussy rubbing against your tongue. And after we both cum I want you take your big dick and fuck me like no tomorrow.

She lifted herself off him, and started at his ankles and slowly licked him up to his ass. She could tell he was enjoying that.

"Turn over," she instructed him. When he did, his hard-on was standing straight up. She knew he liked hearing her talk dirty to him, but it was making her hot, too. Peaches started rubbing oil onto his chest, then his hard, flat stomach. Javon watched her as she continued rubbing his body down.

"You like?" she asked.

Javon nodded. She began to massage his muscular thighs and legs, then, she took his hard-on into her hands and she massaged it. She let one hand go down to his balls and played with them.

Lowering her head, Peaches took him into her mouth. Javon moaned in pleasure. She tongued his shaft down to his sack. She licked and sucked him there, too. Taking him back into her warm mouth, she started working that dick like a dog with a favorite bone. Peaches' head bobbed up and down as she pleased her man.

Javon rolled over to the side, burying his face between her legs. When he began to eat her, her breath caught in her throat. They lay there, both using their mouths to taste each other's most private places. It felt so right, she knew she never wanted to be without Javon.

Peaches pulled herself away from Javon, then, looking him in the eye whispered, "I want you inside me."

She lay back and spread her legs for him. Javon entered her. A thrill ran through her body. He began to stroke her slow and deep. Peaches pulled her legs back farther, until her knees were touching her shoulders. Javon pinned them there, making her completely open to him. He long stroked her, a powerful stroke of his hips on each down stroke, almost as if he were trying to climb inside her. Peaches gazed in his eyes. She felt his passion and drew it to her. Javon's tempo picked up; he rode her in a rhythm of pure lust. He let go of her legs and grabbed her ass. She wrapped her legs around his back and found his rhythm. Their bodies locked in a savage carnal dance of flesh, sweat and grunts. Peaches felt the wave of pleasure flood her body. Trembling, she gripped him even tighter. When Javon also found his release inside her, it only brought her to the verge once again.

Finished, Javon lay on the bed holding her in his arms, but Peaches was insatiable, she licked his chest, sucked on his nipples made her way down between his legs and began raising him back up. Though Javon was spent, Peaches was determined and she was good at pleasing her man. So before long, Javon was ready again. Peaches climbed aboard, straddled him and began riding him to ecstasy.

Today, he was getting her best.

TWENTY | It was early afternoon and KB was standing in front of the building, kicking a few pieces of glass around with his foot.

It had been a month since Derrick had come around. Derrick spotted him as soon as he turned the corner. From the looks of the crowd milling around him, it was obvious he was slinging. Derrick wondered if KB was cut out for the streets or perhaps he had a deep seeded wish to be locked away for life. Either way Derrick was determined that he wouldn't be brought down with him. Derrick sucked his teeth, "Damn, how many times would do I have to tell these fools to not sling on the streets?" Derrick scanned the sidewalk looking for the others, but they weren't in sight. Derrick pulled up down the block and watched from a distance. Something wasn't right; slinging in the open was an invitation for a bust.

He had explained that often enough, cops nowadays had camcorders and all types of surveillance equipment. They could watch for hours, even weeks, gathering evidence, as you stood there, making sale after sale in the open. If you pushed your product through a hole in the wall or a closed door, you didn't run the same risk of any face-to-face with some undercover NARC. That meant no identification to worry about later on. In fact, slinging from behind a closed door meant the only thing you had to worry about was how long the door held up when the task force came. If you had a sturdy door, a few minutes was all you needed to run out the back way or to get rid of the drugs and money. After that, any half-assed lawyer could beat the case. With no drugs, no money and no observation sale, the case was sure to get thrown out.

The problem Derrick knew was that most of these young niggas would rather work the streets than sling from an apartment. It was damn near impossible to keep them inside during the summer. Let's face it; no one wants to spend hours in a hot, stuffy project apartment exchanging drugs through a little hole in the door. But even in the cooler weather, it seemed a lot of these so-called drug dealers would rather work the streets.

That's part of the reason the game was so fucked up. It wasn't about pushing your product and making the money, not anymore; now it was about fame. Niggas had a need to be famous or die trying. They wanted to hustle in the open, let people see them and know their names. As if a block full of fiends was a Hollywood strip. It was nothing to see cats flossing, iced-up and designer down. Driving big cars with gold spinning wheels and shit. It was a hustling "who's who" fashion show. A welcome mat for 5'O and the next thing you know niggas are in front of the judge crying and shit, begging a public defender to find out who snitched on them.

This wasn't the route Derrick wanted to take. If niggas wanted to get knocked on the streets then it was their business, but he had to make sure they kept his name and his money out of it.

Derrick sat in his car for a few minutes, trying to figure out what was going on. He only saw KB, and that was strange. Slinging on the streets was bad enough, but not even having someone to look out or hold you down was asking for trouble. If the cops didn't get you, the stick up kids would.

Satisfied he wasn't going to find out anything sitting in the car, Derrick jumped out the ride, pulled his hat down and walked silently up the block. KB didn't see him until he was about five feet away. The look in KB's eyes told Derrick he'd surprised him. KB probably thought that Derrick was going to stop and question him, but Derrick just walked past him and went into the building.

Derrick hadn't detected any surveillance, but just in case, he wasn't going to make it easy for them by standing in the streets, talking to someone who ten minutes earlier was slinging drugs. 30 seconds later, KB walked into the building looking for Derrick.

"What's up, Dee?" KB sounded unsure, like he was scared or something, and that was enough to put Derrick on point.

"You tell me," Derrick responded, while reaching in his coat pocket to click the safety off his piece.

"I know I'm not supposed to be out here, but I was trying to keep the money flowing. Feel me?" KB said.

Derrick was going to respond, but he started thinking the nigga might be wired. He was acting too funny.

"You ain't wired, is you?" Derrick asked, looking him in the eyes.

"What?" KB stepped back. "Hell no, man, you think I'm working for 5'O? Yo, you know I don't even get down like that. You know how we do it, we family and shit."

"My family serving life in prison."

"Yo," KB frowned, "You like my brother and shit, you know we good kid."

"Just asking. You look kind of nervous."

"It ain't that."

"Then what is it? 'Cause you starting to make my palms sweat." Derrick had his hand on his gun.

"I just ain't want nothing to do with the mess going on upstairs." He was indicating the apartment they sold out of.

"What's going on upstairs?" Derrick asked, but KB didn't respond.

"KB, what's going on upstairs?" Derrick asked for the second time.

"Them niggas got Tasha upstairs," he conceded, reluctantly. "Runnin' a train wreck I guess. 'Cause they got to know that ho is trouble."

Tasha was a chocolate brown, thick-built cutie with a big ass that had a lot of the young boys in the neighborhood, and some of the old heads, scheming on the draws. Two things prevented anyone with good sense from scheming too hard. First, no matter how good she looked, Tasha was only fifteen. Which meant sure enough jail bait. Second, Tasha was a Washington. In fact, Tasha was the baby of the family and the only girl. There were five Washington boys and Mrs. Washington, the matriarch of the family. The oldest of the Washington boys was James, who was at the moment in Clinton Correctional, serving 25 to life for murder. The other four sons were all living in the neighborhood, and were all quick to shoot or stab anyone for the slightest reason. Everyone knew how protective they were over Tasha, so if these fool-ass niggas had her up in the apartment, KB was right, they were runnin' a train wreck.

"Let's go upstairs." Derrick said, insisting that KB lead the way. They walked up the stairs, unlocked the door and stepped into the apartment. Derrick found Tasha naked and bent over a dingy, beige sofa, which besides a cheap wooden table and a few chairs, was the only furniture in the apartment. Red was behind her, pants at his ankles, hands on her hips fucking her from behind. Killa was in front, hands roughly gripping her hair, as his thrusting hips crammed his dick into her mouth. Derrick felt like putting bullets in both these niggas.

"What the fuck y'all doing?"

"Oh shit, Derrick!" Both of them froze, but Tasha kept sucking on Killa's dick, making him have to forcibly pull himself away from her. Derrick walked over to her, grabbed her by her hair and turned her to face him. The look in her eyes told him all he needed to know.

"What she on?" Derrick asked in a harsh whisper.

"It ain't nothing serious, Dee," replied Killa.

"She was just smoking and drinking," Red offered.

"That's it?" Derrick asked, lifting her clothes off the floor and trying to get her dressed.

"We gave her a little EX, you know, just to bring the freak out of her," added Killa. Derrick felt an anger welling up inside him. Yeah, Tasha had a body that looked ripe for fucking, but anyone who looked in her face could see she was just a kid. A kid who, right now, could barely even stand straight, and who obviously didn't even know what the fuck was going on. Derrick didn't even turn to face them, but his voice was clear.

"You two motherfuckas better leave, get out the apartment and get off the block."

"Yo, Dee, we was just having some fun," Killa said.

"Leave, and don't mention this to no one." Derrick turned to face them. "If I hear about this on the streets, you won't have to worry about her brothers coming for you, 'cause I'll deal with you first."

Red turned to leave, but Killa hesitated, then said, "Man, this bitch ain't nobody; besides, we've been working all day. What about our pay?" Killa stared into Derrick's eyes. One thing Derrick understood well was that every confrontation was a test of will. Right now, Killa was testing the seriousness of Derrick's gangsta. Pitting his will against that of Derrick. Derrick smiled; this was the second time this same nigga had tried to intimidate him with that look. Without saying anything Derrick pulled his gun and shot Killa in the thigh. The force of the bullet sent Killa stumbling backwards. He fell hard. Red began moving quickly to the door.

"Red," Derrick pointed the gun at him, "come here!"

"Yo, Dee, I ain't got no beef, cuz. You want me gone, consider me to be the first nigga with wings. I'm out."

"Shut the fuck up!" Derrick spoke with authority. "Now listen to me carefully. Red, I want you to help this nigga up and then leave the area. Both of you niggas done forfeited your pay when you violated the rules," Derrick explained with ice in his voice.

"We wasn't trying to cause no trouble," Red pleaded.

"Money over bitches, Red, you forget that? You niggas let the pussy endanger our operation, and you brought potential beef to our doorstep, not only from her people but from the police, too. The girl is jail bait. You want the police harassing us on some R. Kelly shit? What you think these parents going to be saying if they think we up here fucking their little daughters, getting them high on E? Huh?

"Nigga, when the hood turn against you, you can't get no money, and that's what I'm in this for, the money. Know one thing: the only reason you and this nigga is walking out of here now, is 'cause if I kill one of you, then I got to kill you all, and the problem ain't that serious, yet. But make no mistake about it, if I hear rumors on the streets about what went down in here today, I will come looking for you. Now, help this cripple nigga up and get the fuck off my block!"

Red picked Killa up and helped him hobble out the door with blood trailing behind him. KB was standing off to the side, and Tasha, half-dressed and half-conscious, was sprawled out on the sofa.

"KB, lock the door. We officially closed for the day. Now clean this mother fucker up!"

Derrick finished dressing Tasha and let her sleep it off. He was going to have to stay with her until she sobered up. He would have to convince her that it was in everyone's best interest to forget the whole incident.

It was days like these that Derrick understood Javon's desire to leave the game alone. Too many clowns had infiltrated it. They had no discipline, no principles and no idea how this shit is supposed to be done. The sad part was, these same wannabe gangstas were the first to sell you out when they got trapped off by the law. Soon as the handcuffs closed around their wrist, they were trying to cut a deal and tell on someone. The honor of the street soldier was another commodity sold on the open market.

Derrick looked at the young girl laying on the sofa and shook his head. The game wasn't shit anymore.

Triple Crown Publications presents . . .

TWENTY-ONE | It was one of those big churches with stained glass windows and a large organ, but instead of having a hand painted picture of Jesus and the serving pastor in the lobby, it had photographs of African Kings, Queens and world wide leaders. Yet, it was still something about the church that reminded Javon of the warnings he received from Raheem when he was younger.

"These preachers are rich slave makers of the poor," Raheem would say. "Anytime the congregation is riding on a bus and their preacher is driving Cadillacs, wearing fancy clothes and living in a big house on the hill, things ain't right and exact."

Over the years, Raheem's words always served to deter Javon from places of worship. Yet and still he would attend every now and again; after all, he had often dealt with women who were church goers and to appease them, he might join them at a service, but he never allowed himself to get caught up in all the religious hoopla. As much as he hated to sound cynical, Javon tended to agree with Raheem. He viewed churches as a hustle. Just another way of exploiting the hopes and fears of people who, in most cases, had very little else. In Javon's mind, preachers were just like pimps, which explained why most church congregations were predominately women.

From the crowd of people milling about outside this church, he could tell the congregation here was large. At first, he had been hesitant to come when Fatima had invited him. He had made excuses, but eventually, curiosity had gotten the better of him. Fatima didn't appear to be the type that would be fooled by the common church spiel. Besides, she had insisted it was only a unity service, so he decided to humor her and attend. Standing here now, he knew it would not be the usual kind of religious service.

The crowd outside was anything but the normal church crowd; in fact, they reminded him of the kind of crowd he saw at the Black Expo a few years back. All around were people decked out in African gear. Other, more conservative types were draped in business suits, having craftily Africanized their attire with Kente cloth, handkerchiefs and other accessories. You had the jeans and hoodies crowd in attendance as well. The one apparent constant among the crowd was the black beads they all wore. Everywhere you looked, they had on black beaded necklaces from which hung one of those Ankhs.

Javon had often seen Fatima wearing similar beads, and of course, he had always attributed it to her level of black consciousness. Now, seeing so many people all wearing the same black beads obviously meant it was no simple curio.

Javon scanned the crowd and found Fatima near the entrance. He made his way toward her.

Fatima was immersed in a conversation with Aaliyah. She turned and saw Javon coming her way. She smiled, pleasantly surprised that he had showed up. To tell the truth, he had been on her mind lately, which disturbed her a little. Although she found him attractive, Fatima had no intention of mixing up her business plans with any relationship. She had learned the hard way the pain you could bring yourself to when you let your guard down. She didn't get the feeling that Javon was out to manipulate her in any way, but she was far from the innocent little girl she once was, so she was on point anyway.

"Hotep, brotha, I'm glad to see you could finally make it. This is my sista, Aaliyah," Fatima introduced Aaliyah.

"Hello," Javon replied, "it's good to meet you." he shook hands with Aaliyah.

"My pleasure," Aaliyah responded, eyeing Javon appreciatively, then, facing Fatima with a big, silly grin and eye signals.

Blushing, and hoping that Javon hadn't seen Aaliyah's facial theatrics, Fatima quickly spoke up. "So I'm glad you could take the time to join us."

"Well, I was dying to see what this unity service was all about."

"Good." Aaliyah wrapped her arms around Javon's. "You can sit with me and Fatima. We'll make sure you don't miss a thing. Ain't that right Fatima?"

Fatima looked at her thinking, *This girl has no shame.* Yet, she followed Aaliyah and Javon into the temple.

Sitting in between Fatima and Aaliyah, Javon rapidly realized that the girls were well known and well loved among the congregation. It seemed as if every person that passed by took the opportunity to greet them or share with them a few friendly words.

When the service began, it didn't take long for Javon to become engrossed in the happenings. He had never been to a service like this before. The choir, which was called Nubian Voices, sang spiritual and motivational songs; not really church music, although it had that gospel feel. The songs were secular, like "Black Butterfly" by Denise Williams, or, "I Believe I Can Fly" by R. Kelly.

After the choir had gotten the congregation into the right mood, the priest came forward to perform a libation and to light some candles. Though he spoke in a language Javon couldn't make out, he was courteous enough to translate at certain junctures of the ritual. From what Javon could make out, it was a tribute to the ancestors.

Following that, the priest began his sermon. Javon listened raptly. The priest had a speaking style similar to Louis Farrakhan. Anyone who had ever heard Farrakhan speak knew he preached religion wrapped in reality. That's the way this priest was giving it up. "My brothas and my sistas," the pastor said, "we are in a world where we must love one another, be there for one another, but at the same time keep it real with each other. Don't condone your brother sleeping around with three different women and then act as if the babies he makes don't exist or act as if AIDS is not a possibility. We have to remember that we are responsible for one another, each one must teach one. And to our sisters you must treat your body as a temple ..." And on he went on. By the time he had concluded his sermon he'd preached about poverty, crime, stories of strength, wisdom, the beauty of black people and how only sticking together would black people overcome adversity. He gave the people something to believe in, filling them with hope for a better tomorrow.

The priest spoke for nearly two hours, and by the time he was done, the congregation was in a state of elation. An aura of pride, love and unity enveloped everyone. It was a warmth Javon hadn't felt since he was a child spending time with his mother and Raheem.

That's when the choir made its way back out. This time, the lead singer taking the microphone was Fatima. Javon had noticed her leave her seat moments before, but had been so engrossed in the sermon that he'd paid it little attention. Now she had his and everyone else's attention.

Fatima started low, her voice barely a whisper, her eyes closed, as if she were in a trance. Then, her sound grew, pushing from inside her. Her vocals traversing the temple, weaving itself into the aura of unity that permeated the place. The air itself became electric. Her voice caused goose bumps on Javon's skin. The congregation began to sing with her. Javon turned and saw Aaliyah caught up in the rapture that was Fatima's voice. Everywhere Javon turned, the people who had gathered at the temple on this day were mesmerized by Fatima.

Javon knew in part it had been the sermon, the music, and the service which had made the people comfortable with each other. Love was in the air, and not just any love, but black love. In the reality most people face, day to day, that was a rare commodity. Yet, Javon knew it was also more than that. It was Fatima. She had a genuine talent that kept the listener in awe of her gift. If Javon had ever had doubts about her ability, they no longer existed. Fatima was headed for superstardom, and the thought brought Javon relief.

Triple Crown Publications presents . . .

TWENTY-TWO | Javon pulled into the parking

garage below the Shriver building. The Shriver building was a Midtown high-rise which housed amongst numerous other business offices, the business office of the newly formed Keynote Records. In four months, Craig had succeeded in putting together his vision of a new label. Along with Charles Jackson and Javon Williams, they had established Keynote Records, and already they were faced with problems.

Javon found a parking spot and hastily made his way to the elevators. He had caught the news on the radio that morning. Between that and the tidbits he'd gotten from Craig last night, or better said, earlier this morning, because Craig had called at three in the morning, Javon could piece together enough to know that G-Rydah and his boys had gotten into a shootout with some rapper from Street Life Records. He could imagine the chaos the office would be in this morning. As Javon made his way to Craig's office, all eyes were on him. By the somber looks, he could tell that word of the incident had spread.

Javon arrived at Lori's desk. She had been Craig's secretary since he started in the business. She was always organized, efficient and professional. Even now, you would never tell something was amiss by the cool mannerisms she displayed.

"Is Craig in?" Javon asked.

"Yes, Mr. Williams. He's expecting you."

Javon knocked on the door, then walked in. Craig was seated

at his desk with the phone cradled between his chin and shoulder, as he scribbled some notes on a piece of paper. Javon took a seat across from him and waited. Craig looked as if he hadn't slept all night, which was probably the case. His disheveled looks and bleary eyes told Javon he'd probably spent all morning trying to iron out whatever problems would inevitably arise from this latest incident.

When he concluded his phone call, Craig breathed a heavy sigh and lowered his head to the desk. The way his shoulders were slumped, it seemed he carried the weight of the world on his shoulders.

"What's the damage, Craig?" Javon asked. Craig looked up, his eyes meeting Javon's before he spoke.

"Maybe you can explain something to me, 'cause I don't get it. I mean, I didn't grow up with a silver spoon in my mouth but I can't say that I lived the life that these rap kids brag about, either. Still, I thought the point was to make some money so you could change your condition for the better. So please, explain to me why this kid, who just went platinum, and who is about to become the biggest thing on the Hip Hop scene, is going to fuck his whole life up by going into a club and getting into a shoot out? Explain that to me. You're more knowledgeable in these things than me. So tell me, what the fuck was this kid thinking?"

Javon understood Craig's frustration. He had invested a lot in this kid. Not only money, but time and energy, also. In seemed every kid in the hood was looking to the mic as a way out of the ghetto, but few ever made it. Craig had seen the potential in G-Rydah, and had nourished it. Sure, the kid was talented, but the streets, the prisons and the graveyards were filled with talented people who never got the opportunity to shine. Craig had given him that opportunity and G-Rydah was on the verge of tossing it all away.

"What did the police say?" Javon asked.

"They're investigating. So far, they haven't charged G-Rydah with anything, but the other one, Darren Wesley, has been charged with the shooting."

"Who's Darren Wesley?"

"The skinny kid with the braids that always be with G-Rydah."

"Oh, you're talking about Dee-Dawg."

"Yeah, Dee-Dawg. Anyway word is G-Rydah passed him the gun. Which if it proves true, makes him an accomplice. The one good thing is the kid from Street Life Records didn't die. He's in the hospital with four bullet holes in his body. "

"So how do we fix this?"

"I spoke with Rasheed Collins over at Street Life. He wants to meet with me later on this afternoon. I had a meeting earlier with Charles and he's pretty upset. He runs a low-key label, basically because he deals with jazz artists. He's not accustomed to this thug life mentality most of the modern rappers want to live out. Anyway, the lawyers have been dealing with the police and I told my assistant, Johnny, to keep an eye on G-Rydah. We need to baby-sit him so he doesn't do anything stupid while we're trying to get all this straightened out."

"Well, tell me if you need me to do anything," Javon offered, but really wasn't sure what he could do. Until the police decided what they were going to do, it was all a waiting game.

"You know the funny thing?" Craig asked, smiling at the irony of it all. "If he does get charged, the publicity of it all would probably guarantee him going double platinum. As crazy as it sounds, he's a gangsta rapper, so he is doing exactly what the fans expect a gangsta to do."

Javon considered Craig's last statement. G-Rydah was becoming the persona he rapped about in his music. Unfortunately, when you trade in spitting lyrics for spitting shells, you better know what you're doing. One thing's for certain, a hot sixteen does a lot more damage when they're coming out of the barrel of a gun.

TWENTY-THREE | A week had passed since

Fatima had last seen Javon. She paid the cab driver, jumped out and made her way to her apartment building. She was juggling her big carry-all bag with one hand, as she dug into it with the other, looking for her keys. Tired, hungry and sore, she stepped into the apartment. The photo shoot had lasted three hours. She'd also done three interviews. Not to mention another four hours in the studio putting the finishing touches on her tracks.

She wasn't complaining. She knew this was part of the drill. The 6:00 wake ups, the ten or twelve hours working to get the music right, the photo shoots and interviews with reporters that ask the same questions over and over again. The more fame and money you wanted, the more time and effort you had to put in. Right now, Fatima was making it through on adrenaline.

Fatima made her way to the bathroom. The plan was simple. A nice hot soak in the tub, then she planned on putting on her night shirt and hitting the bed for a few hours, though a few days would probably feel better.

While the tub was filling up, she stepped into the kitchen and got herself some fruit cocktail to snack on, then went into the bedroom and checked her messages. Aaliyah's voice came through, reminding her that tonight was sister circle night. Fatima loved her Nubian sisters, but she sure did not feel like going to session tonight. However, she knew if she didn't show up, Mama Safiya would throw a fit. She was already complaining about Fatima missing too many services.

Fatima was fed up with their attitude toward her musical career. It didn't slip Fatima's attention that whenever she sang or did some benefit for the lodge, Mama Safiya had no problem, but let the talk turn to furthering her career in the Industry, and all of a sudden, she wanted to preach about responsibility and giving back to the community. Fatima didn't have anything against giving back, and she had done more then her share in that department. But the burden of people always expecting more from you had been placed on her since birth. She just wanted to be Fatima, and sing for no other reason than she loved to sing.

Besides, she didn't like Mama Safiya always in her business. She was always questioning who Fatima was out with and she never really believed her, even when Fatima told her the truth. Fact is, Fatima had dated a few men, but had not been in a serious relationship since Solomon. The thought of Solomon always brought back wonderful memories, and tragic ones, too.

Solomon came into Fatima's life when she was at her lowest. It was the period right after she had tried to commit suicide. She was sent to the hospital. The doctors told her aunt it was a case of severe depression. Everybody felt it was unnatural for a girl so young to be suffering from depression, but they didn't understand her life. How was she supposed to feel? She'd lost her Mama, and her Baba had sent her away to live with strangers. Just living in America was hard in itself. In Africa, even the strangers you met on the road were courteous. Here, in America, people either ignored you or were rude for no reason.

The greatest injury of all was believing that God had chosen her to bless the world with song. Ever since Fatima was a little girl and witnessed Mama's magic and saw how she affected everyone she came into contact with through the power of her voice, all Fatima dreamed about was one day being able to do the same thing. Instead, her dreams were shattered by a man who used her like a prostitute, then tossed her aside. Depression wasn't even deep enough for how she felt. Each day was just another opportunity to live with the shame that haunted her.

That was when she met Aaliyah. She worked in the hospital and was a couple of years older than Fatima, but they bonded easily. Aaliyah would come spend time with Fatima every day and bring her books and magazines. She loved the fact that Fatima was from Africa.

Aaliyah was on a cultural kick. She wore a black beaded necklace with an ankh for a pendant. Fatima thought it was silly how black people in America always wanted to associate wearing Kente cloth and African trinkets as being in touch with their heritage. Still, Aaliyah was different; she really cared about people, and Fatima sensed her sincerity immediately.

Fatima could still remember the first time Aaliyah dragged her to one of the services at the temple. Fatima argued that she was a Muslim, but Aaliyah kept telling her it didn't matter; the temple was about black unity through spiritual belief, no matter what your spiritual belief was. When they finally arrived at the temple, Fatima was amazed. It was an African worship service. The High Priest was dressed up in a long flowing robe. The temple was decorated in ancient African symbols like the Ankh, pyramids and the eye of Hero.

When the service started, the High Priest touched upon their common descent from African roots and their need for unity in order to be resurrected as a people. The clear emphasis on spirituality was in getting in touch with God, however one acknowledged God. It was a strange experience, but for the first time since leaving Tanzania, Fatima felt a common black respect and love in the atmosphere.

At the end of the service, she met Aaliyah's siblings. Her sister, Brooklyn, and her brother, Solomon. Solomon was brown-skinned, slim but well built, and had the most beautiful eyes

Fatima had ever seen. They were dark and piercing like he was looking right into her soul. When he smiled Fatima was lost.

"Fatima, this is my brother, Solomon," Aaliyah introduced them.

"How are you doing sista?" His voice was deep and smooth.

"I'm fine, thank you." Fatima was tongue tied and nervous.

"You have a beautiful accent. Are you from the West Indies?" he asked her.

"No, Tanzania."

"Africa?! You serious? Well, it's a pleasure to meet a sister from the motherland." Fatima felt proud, although she knew she hadn't done anything to be proud of, still, that Solomon was pleased to meet her, pleased her.

"Thank you." Fatima was sure she sounded ignorant, but she really was at a loss for words. Looking back at it now, she knew she had sounded like some idiot foreigner, and the thought made her laugh. She, Brooklyn and Solomon all became friends. Yet she and Solomon became a lot more. They became each other's greatest love and worst obsession.

TWENTY-FOUR | Javon and Derrick were in the
back room of the Fulton Street Club having a sit down with True
God and two of his boys. Most of the people in the club who were
paying attention probably thought it was another drug transaction
taking place. After all, it was no secret that True God had half of
Fort Greene under control. They were making paper, hand over
fist. However, this meeting wasn't about drugs at all. It was about
the music business. Since the shooting incident at the night club,
Craig had met with Rasheed, the CEO of Street Life Records,
three times, but nothing had been resolved. Street Life Records
was a low level independent label trying to come up in the music
industry. The CEO was a locally known DJ, and party promoter,
who had yet to grind out that one hit he needed to propel himself
upward.

The shooting of one of his artists by a member of G-Rydah's
entourage was too good an opportunity for him not to try to milk
it. G-Rydah is a platinum-selling recording artist that meant
money. It was obvious that Rasheed had plans on shaking Craig
down for a share. Javon realized what Rasheed was trying to do,
and started to look into the matter himself. What he found was
that the money man behind Street Life Records was True God.

Javon and Derrick both knew True God from past dealings
and neither of them liked him. Though it may be true, there's no
honor amongst thieves, True God gave the word grimey a deeper
meaning. Nonetheless, they called True God up and scheduled

this meeting.

"What's up, Gee? Y'all looking to do some business?" True asked.

"Yeah," Javon responded, "but not on the drug tip, we got something else we want to kick with you."

"If it's about money, black man, then you got my attention," True replied.

"It's about Street Life Records," Javon informed him.

"Oh, yeah, what about it, Gee?"

"I heard you might have some influence over there and we're trying to resolve a little something with them."

"Well, I don't know about all that, but talk to me. What's up?" True God leaned back in his seat, crossing his arms on his chest.

"A couple of weeks ago, one of your boys, L-Boogie, got shot at a night club. He told the police that one of our guys was the one who allegedly shot him."

"Yeah, I heard about that."

"Well, we'd like the kid to tell the police that in all the confusion of the shooting, he pointed out the wrong guy ... feel me?"

"Yeah, I feel you Gee; the thing is, all that music shit, that's the God Ra's operation. I ain't got shit to do with that," True God explained.

Up until that moment Derrick had chosen to remain silent and see how things turned out, but the more he listened, the more aggravated he became. These fools were sitting here discussing all this business shit, and neglecting the fact that L-Boogie was a rat and Rasheed was trying to profit from his telling.

"True," Derrick interjected, "I'm with you on this music shit. I don't know nothing about it and don't give a fuck about it. But I do know bad business when I see it. The kid L-Boogie is a rat, straight like that. He told the police who shot him and your man Rasheed is trying to hit us up for paper, claiming he's trying to keep G-Rydah's name out of it. So keeping it real, your boy is trying to play us."

"Nah, it ain't like that, black man. The God Ra is trying to make sure we don't take no losses. We got money tied up in this thing and our artist is shot up. We got to pay his hospital bills, and in the meanwhile, we ain't seeing nothing coming in 'cause he ain't in no shape to perform. We the ones looking at a loss, here," True God tried to argue.

"Homie, it ain't about the money," Derrick told him. And it wasn't, at least not to Derrick. Derrick was a hustler, so he understood the paper aspect of it all, but in spite of that, he didn't encourage a nigga snitching. That's why the game was so fucked up. A lot of niggas getting money on the streets were certified snitches, still, supposedly real niggas turned a blind eye to it. As long as niggas got paid, they were willing to let a snitch live. In Derrick's opinion, this kid Rasheed was a foul nigga. He knew that L-Boogie already had D-Dawg fighting a case, and now, he wanted to get paid to keep G-Rydah out the mix.

"The point is, you harboring a snitch-ass nigga," Derrick stated.

"Word is bond, don't even come at me like that. I already told you Rasheed run that."

"Well, you need to check him about that. You want to talk about money, then check this out. The whole incident got police investigating Street Life Records, as well as Keynote Records. We all got shit invested. Same way you don't like taking losses, we don't either. Especially, 'cause some fake-ass, wankster-nigga don't know how to keep his fucking mouth shut."

"So what you saying?" True God was upset.

"I'm saying, we know how to close a nigga's mouth for good!" Derrick eyed True God challengingly, and the table became silent.

"Okay, breathe easy," Javon finally spoke up, trying to ease the tension that was building.

"Yo, Gee," True God turned to speak with Javon, "I came to

build with y'all about some paper, and your boy coming at me on some gangsta shit."

"Don't get it twisted, nigga, this is some gangsta shit. You in the presence of real gangstas," Derrick replied.

He was ready to put an end to this conversation. As far as he was concerned, it wasn't going anywhere, and he didn't have the patience for it. He had basically come to give Javon a hand, but the whole episode was starting to leave him with a sour taste in his mouth. It was simple to him. L-Boogie was a rat, and if you fucked with a rat, you'd probably eat cheese, too.

"We ain't getting nowhere like this," Javon stated, "so let's start over. I got an offer to put on the table. You say you paying the hospital bills and ain't seeing nothing in return right? So, it's basically a money thing."

"That's all I'm saying. As long as we see our paper, everything is gravy ... feel me?"

"Okay, this is what we can do. You get L-Boogie to tell the D.A. he ain't sure it was D-Dawg that shot him, and Rasheed to pull back from trying to blow this up in every fucking interview he makes, and we'll push a half a brick your way."

"A half a brick?"

"Yeah, that will cover hospital bills and still make you a profit."

"Yeah, but what I need more product for? You know I got my own shit."

"Because it's free, and because we paying you to do something that you should be doing anyway. Let's face it, no matter what we say, it's about more than money. It's also about a nigga keeping his reputation clean. What L-Boogie did ain't right. We both know that. This way, you get a chance to straighten all that out and it don't cost you a thing. You make a little money, our boy gets out, and everybody's happy... feel me?"

"Yeah, I feel you. Okay, I'm going to straighten this bullshit out, 'cause the God don't get down like that."

"All right, so everything is good, right?"

"Yeah, we straight, black man."

"Okay, take this number." Javon passed True God a slip of paper. "They'll be expecting your call. Everything will be ready."

Javon stood up to leave and reached over to shake True God's hand. Derrick also stood up, but he had no intention of shaking hands with anyone. It wasn't his style. So he just made his way to the door and let Javon handle all the kid glove bullshit. If these niggas didn't like it, he wasn't hard to find.

Triple Crown Publications presents . . .

TWENTY-FIVE | Javon entered Craig's office to

find him pouring over some paperwork. His first thought was of how much Craig was starting to look the part of a stressed-out business executive. Neither one of them were past the age of thirty, yet Craig was already balding on the top, getting flabby around the middle, and had the continuous look of concern on his face, as if every event was the end of the world. Javon wondered how often Craig spent time with his wife and kids. One thing was certain, Javon had no intention of becoming one of these obsessive workaholics that somewhere down the line shot themselves in the head because they had no life outside of work.

"What's up, Craig?" Javon asked, taking a seat. Craig re-adjusted the paperwork on his desk, sat back, then ran his fingers through his sparse hair, and exhaled a sigh of exasperation. He had that haggard look of a man who had seen little sleep in days.

"Well, Javon, I wanted to talk with you about our future." Craig eyed Javon seriously. "I've been doing a lot of thinking. You know how I am, always trying to figure out the best angles. Anyway, I came up with some conclusions I wanted to run by you."

"Sure," Javon replied. Craig had peaked his curiosity.

"Well, first I want to thank you for handling the situation with D-Dawg and the fellas over at Street Life Records."

"That's nothing. We're all in this together."

"Yeah, we are, and that's the point, Javon. The music business isn't the same as it once was. It has become so street oriented that sometimes I think more deals are made under the tables than they are in the boardrooms."

Javon could understand that. He even agreed with the assessment. In the few months he had been with Craig and Charles, he had come in contact with enough music executives and producers to see that each one of them had some link with the streets. If you were in the music business, especially the rap game, and didn't connect with the streets, you had no credibility and little influence.

"Anyway," Craig continued, "the point is, I probably wouldn't have been able to defuse the problem without your help. Unfortunately, right now I'm faced with another problem that I need your advice on. And while I was thinking about it, I came to the realization that we're going to have to stay in tune with the times. If we look at it reasonably, each one of us brings something to the label. I mean, let's face it, I can deal with some of the older music execs, but these new young producers and label owners... I just can't reach them. At least, not in the way you can. So, what I want to do is talk with Charles and find a way for you to take a more active role in the label. That is if you're up to the job."

Javon wanted to take on more responsibility at the label, but he just wasn't sure exactly what Craig expected. The reason he had been the silent in the group was specifically because of his connection to the streets. He didn't need or want questions about his finances coming up.

"I thought my involvement in the streets would bring too many unwanted inquiries," Javon responded.

"That's just it, Javon; in the old days, guys like you were taboo. Not to say they weren't around, because they were. But they stayed out of the limelight. The big boys made sure not to soil their hands with anyone of questionable background. But with Jay Z, Suge Knight, Master P and even those Cash Money guys, the industry is showing them they don't care about their history or your street affiliations, as long as you can push them units. If you can make those millions," Craig explained, "they don't care."

But Javon still was not convinced. It was not too long ago that Irv Gotti and Murda Inc had been under investigation for alleged affiliations to the drug game. Of course, Javon had always managed to stay below the radar with his illegal activities. Yet, it was precisely because he was careful, precisely because he avoided the limelight, that he was not on the police hot sheet. Javon felt safe being a silent partner, but how much trouble could he get himself into if he took a more active role? As he thought about it, he realized he had come to a crossroad.

It nagged him that Craig had identified him as "guys like you." In other words, though Javon ran a club and was already a partner in the label, he was still viewed as an outsider. Not as a businessman, which he obviously was, but as someone of ill repute.

Unfortunately, Javon also realized that his own hesitancy was acquiescence of that identity. If he was really trying to get out of the game and go legit, it wouldn't matter if he took a more visible role, since there would be no more need for remaining hidden. Was his reluctance a sign he really wasn't ready to leave the game? Was he just fooling himself? NO! He decided it was time to step up. The transition had to start somewhere, and this was a good a place as any.

"Yeah, I'm ready for some more responsibility," he assured Craig.

"Good," Craig replied, moving around the desk to come shake hands with Javon, "'cause we got a problem."

"What did G-Rydah do now?" asked Javon.

"No," Craig responded. "It's Fatima."

Triple Crown Publications presents . . .

TWENTY-SIX | "Fatima is what?!" Javon couldn't

believe what he was hearing.

"Javon, she part of a cult—one of those militant cults, like them crazy-ass white folks in Waco, Texas, except this one's a black cult."

Javon couldn't help his laughter. Although he knew Craig was serious, the idea that Craig was so out of touch with what was going on around the hood was hilarious. Craig, however, did not see what Javon found so funny.

"What are you laughing at? It's not a joke, Javon. I have it from a reliable source. She's tied into one of them black militant cults," Craig said, somewhat annoyed at Javon's levity.

"Craig, I don't mean to laugh, but you should see the look on your face." Javon tried to regain his composure, but tears still streamed from his eyes.

"The look on my face is the look of a man who has put a lot of work into this project and stands to lose a lot of money because one of the main talents on this label is some crazy black militant member." Craig was angry and it showed.

"Okay, okay, take it easy. First of all, she's not part of some crazy cult. She's a Nubian sista. She attends that Nubian Temple down in Crown Heights, Brooklyn. They ain't no crazy militants, they just black conscious people. I've been to the temple myself. They're normal black folks. You can trust me on that one."

"You've been there?"

"Yeah, it's just a bunch of black folks discussing black issues and celebrating African culture," Javon explained.

"Well, from what I hear, they're down with some underground terrorist group trying to start a race war in America."

"Craig, you're reading too much into it. It ain't like that."

"Oh, yeah? Do you know who her father is?" Craig asked.

"I think she told me she was born in Africa." Javon replied.

"Oh, she was, but her father was born here, and he happens to be one of America's most wanted," Craig responded smugly.

"You're kidding?" Craig had his attention now.

"No, I'm serious. Her father's name is Leroy Jenkins and he's been on the run in Africa for years."

Javon recognized the name immediately. "You're talking about THE LEROY JENKINS ... Kareem Amir ... Leroy Jenkins, the Black Panther?"

"Yeah, that's the same guy."

"Oh, shit." Javon was stunned.

Leroy Jenkins had been one of the most well known Black Panthers of his time. After the death of Fred Hampton and Mark Clark at the hands of the Chicago police, Leroy Jenkins had been charged with retaliating in an ambush of his own, leaving two police officers shot; one fatally. When the pressure came down on him, he skipped town, turning up years later in Africa, where he stayed living in exile. To learn that Fatima was his daughter was amazing to Javon.

"So, you think they're still normal black folks? Javon, it's not a coincidence that her old man happens to be one of America's most wanted and she's involved in a group with ties to terrorists."

Javon was no longer laughing. In fact, he was slightly annoyed with Craig.

"Leroy Jenkins ain't no criminal. The man was one of the most well known Panthers of the era. He's a legend in Chicago, and in the black community."

"Well, that's a matter of opinion, and in the opinion of those who matter, namely the government of the United States of America, he's a criminal on the run in Africa."

"You know what Craig, you're a hypocrite. I remember how you were making a big deal about Ice Cube's movie disrespecting a black icon like Rosa Parks. But now you sit here calling another black icon a common criminal."

"I'm just saying what's going to be put out there. My concern is Fatima. She's got talent and she's going to be a star. So, all this is bound to come out. We have to be ready to deal with it."

"What's the big deal? Like you said, this business don't care about your history as long as you can make the big dollars."

"That's different. I was talking about us, the guys behind the scene. The business doesn't care about our history, at least not like it used to. But she's an artist. She has to worry about what the public thinks. You'd be surprised how much pressure the police fraternities can exert."

"You think they'd do that?" Javon asked.

"Probably. The police don't like Panthers or their children."

"I know, but that didn't stop Tupac from success," Javon reasoned.

"Tupac was different; he was a rapper. The controversy actually ly helped him. And the fact that his people were Panthers gave credence to his lyrics. Fatima's an R&B soul singer, and besides, her father is wanted for cop killing. That's the kind of thing where they pull out the cop's family and kids and parade them around to garner sympathy. You know, cop's kids–victims. Killer's kid–famous star. It's a probability that if Fatima's CD does good, and I'm bettin' it will, we're going to be faced with an onslaught of controversy. With her ties to the Nubian Temple, and the rumors that circulate around that place, it might just damage her chances of ever becoming as big a star as she could be."

Though Craig made it seem he was worried about Fatima,

Javon knew he was more concerned with the money he had invested in her. He didn't blame him though; no one got into business to lose money.

"So, how do you think we should handle it?" Javon asked.

"You seem to have hit it off well with her, so maybe she'll listen to you. Explain the situation to her; let her know what to expect and what's on the line. In the end, the choices are hers, but we're all going to feel the effects of her decisions. We all got a lot invested."

"I'll do what I can to make sure she understands what's at stake."

"That's all I'm asking."

TWENTY-SEVEN | Peaches was uptight. Hell, she

was beyond uptight. This wasn't the first time Javon had stood her up. Over the last three months, she had been seeing less and less of him. Ever since he started running with those people in the music industry, he didn't have time for her anymore. The funny thing was, at first, Peaches had encouraged him. Fuck that supporting your man shit. She was simply thinking that he could get her some work in the music videos. But just the opposite was happening. Javon was hanging out with Rap stars and Peaches was still stripping at the club and going nowhere.

Worst of all were nights like tonight, when her girl wanted to go out on a double date party night, and she was stuck without a man to call her own. What was that all about? Peaches rolled a blunt, picked up the phone and called Sandra.

"Yeah, what's up, girl?" Sandra answered.

"Hey Sandra, how'd you know it was me?" Peaches could hear loud music blaring in the background.

"Girl, you serious? I caller ID everybody before I answer. So what's up? You and cutie pie on the way over?"

"Nah, Javon can't come. He's taking care of business."

"What!? That nigga ain't coming to hang out on my birthday? Peaches, you better cuss his ass out for sure."

"Girl, you know I am. Anyway, I just called so you wouldn't be sitting around waiting on us."

"What you mean, 'us'? I know you still coming, right?"

"I don't want to be no third wheel. You going to have your man with you. You and me can celebrate on the weekend."

"Hell no! I want to celebrate tonight! And please, bitch, don't be running that 'your man' shit. This nigga is coming along so I ain't got to pay for shit; but you, you my girl, you better not flip on me now."

"What am I supposed to do while you all up under that nigga?"

"Who you fooling? You ain't been having no problem getting niggas to pay attention to you. When we hit the club and you shake that ass, you going to have every nigga in there sweating you and you know it, so knock off the bullshit and come on over." Peaches had to laugh. That was Sandra. She never took no for an answer.

An hour later, Peaches had driven over to Sandra's house. She lived in one of those beautiful brownstones—the old ones with the high ceilings and hard wood floors. It even had a fireplace. It was a pretty big place for just her and Lil' Man. Lil' Man was her eight-year-old son. His name was really Robert, but he was so smart and serious all the time that he was like a little man. A lot of times, between Lil' Man and Sandra, it was hard to tell who was the parent and who was the child. Lil' Man wasn't home tonight. He was with his father. Peaches envied Sandra, in that, although her and her baby daddy weren't together, he was still around to take care of his child.

Sandra's partner for the night was this tall, good looking, chocolate brother named Tony.

Sandra had met him at the club while she was dancing. That was Sandra. She had no hesitation about going out with a guy she met at the club. Peaches didn't agree. It was like some unwritten rule she didn't want to break. Peaches felt if a guy met you in the club half-naked, then to him, you were always a stripper. Sooner or later, when the novelty of fucking a stripper wore off, most guys would bounce in a hurry. After all, who wanted a relationship with a stripper? Most guys couldn't handle it, but Sandra didn't care.

Once Peaches asked her, "Don't you think the guys that meet you in the club just think of you as a stripper?"

Sandra looked at her like she was crazy and answered, "I am a stripper." That was the end of the conversation as far as she was concerned. Peaches couldn't help thinking that Sandra might be a little wild at times, but tonight, she had her man to take her out and Peaches didn't even know where her man was, so who was really on top of her game?

Sandra, Peaches and Tony hopped into Tony's Escalade and made their way to this club in Midtown. Once inside, they made their way to the VIP section where Tony knew quite a few people. You could tell he was trying to impress Sandra, and it was all good. He kept that table loaded with bottles of Cristal and paid for everything.

Both Peaches and Sandra had come dressed to kill. Peaches had on these Prada jeans that had every male, and even some females in there taking second looks. Sandra had on a Dolce & Gabbana catsuit that fit her every curve like it was part of her skin. She was bound to be in a few niggas' dreams tonight.

Sandra played Tony close, which made him feel like he was the man, and for tonight, he was.

Peaches hit the dance floor and gave a few different guys some conversation, but her mind was on Javon. She kept asking herself, *Am I losing my man, or what?* Javon had accepted her being a stripper from the start. So she knew it wasn't that. But things were changing between them and she could feel it. Sandra must have sensed Peaches' distraction, so she stepped up to disrupt her thoughts.

"Girl, come with me to the bathroom." They made their way to the ladies' room, leaving Tony at the table with a "be right back" and a kiss on the cheek.

"Girl, what's up? You ain't even trying to have any fun."

"I'm straight, Sandra, I'm just chillin'."

"Fuck chillin'. You see all them niggas trying to holler at you? Girl, you got some bona-fide ballers in this place. You better snatch up some digits."

"I ain't even thinking about these niggas. I'm here to hang out with you."

"Okay, I feel that, but don't let no opportunity pass you by. That tall brother with the bald head that was trying to talk to you plays ball for the New Jersey Nets. If you bag him, you good to go... feel me?"

Peaches had to smile. Sandra was a trip sometimes, but that was her girl. They freshened up in the bathroom mirror, then stopped by the bar to get a stronger drink. If they were going to party, might as well party right.

"Can I buy you ladies a drink?" This young-ass wannabe playa was trying to holler at them.

"You sure you can handle it, sweetie?" Sandra said teasingly.

"I think so!"

He pulled out a big knot of cash. From the platinum Rolex watch and chain the young nigga was wearing, he definitely had some deep pockets.

"Who's talking about the drinks?" Sandra smirked, then winked at him.

Just like that, Sandra had the nigga's undivided attention.

"I can handle anything you throw my way."

Shorty sounded confident, but he didn't know Sandra. Peaches smiled to herself as Sandra worked him. He may have thought he was laying his mack down, but he would soon find out he was way out of his league. Sandra ate niggas like him for breakfast. She took his number, and then Peaches and Sandra made their way back to the table where Tony still sat.

For the rest of the night, they partied like there was no tomorrow. Sometimes, you got to live for the moment. So, Peaches pushed Javon to the back of her mind and got her groove on. Tonight, it was just her and her girl.

Triple Crown Publications presents . . .

TWENTY-EIGHT | Fatima, the producer and the engineer, sat in the studio listening to her voice pump out the speaker. They had been working on this last song for almost four hours. Of course, this was no ordinary song. This was the title track, and Fatima's tribute to her mother. She wanted it to be perfect.

"The drum beats ain't sitting right on this track." The engineer was at the board trying to get the track to sit right behind Fatima's voice without distracting her from her song.

"I can tell," Fatima agreed. "They're not right for this song."

"It's not that, Fatima. Your voice is strong enough to make it work. It's just that the drums are competing with you. We need something in between that will help it all blend together," the producer explained.

"We could do some background vocals and fade it in," the engineer suggested.

"Yeah, but she's done that on a number of her songs already. We want something that will make this song stand out. Something bigger. Remember, this song is all heart and soul. "

"How about going with a full choir background?" the engineer offered.

"That's a good idea, but we have to keep it from getting too gospel. What do you think, Fatima?" the producer asked.

"A choir sounds good to me," Fatima stated, willing to give the idea a go.

The studio door suddenly opened and in walked Craig and Javon, engrossed in their own conversation. Craig broke off the conversation and sauntered over to the group.

"How's it going?" he asked. Everyone knew the question wasn't a personal inquiry. He meant how was the song coming along. Craig was focused like that. He didn't waste time on pleasantries when his mind was on business.

While the producer ran down the situation and what they had been working on, Javon slid over to where Fatima stood and spoke to her.

"How you coming along?"

"I'm good, working all day, but still loving every minute of it."

Fatima couldn't help but smile whenever Javon was near. He had a way of making her feel comfortable.

"I heard the tracks you put together so far, and they sound pretty good. I was talking to Craig and he says your CD should debut in the top 20," Javon informed her.

"I hope so, because we've been working really hard on it."

Fatima and Javon found themselves in a conversation of their own. For weeks now, they both had sensed a level of attraction between them, but for their own reasons, each of them was hesitant to pursue it. Javon, for his part, did not want to involve himself with anyone until he could disentangle himself from the drug trade. Though he liked Fatima, he did not know how she would react if she knew about his dealings in the streets. To tell the truth, he was in no hurry to find out. As for Fatima, she had made the mistake of allowing things to go down this road once before, and in the end, it had become the road to hell. Fatima liked Javon also, but she wanted her career first and foremost. More importantly, she needed her career to be about her music and nothing else. If after that goal had been reached, she and Javon could find a space for them amongst all the madness, then she would be willing, but not now. Now she had too much on the line.

"Can we go outside? I need to speak to you privately," Javon said.

"Privately?" Fatima questioned.

"Well, it's really business, but not something that needs to be discussed in front of everyone."

"Okay, let me see if they need me to do any more vocals." Fatima walked toward Craig and the other two men.

Javon had to admit, the possibility of a relationship with Fatima was on his mind. Though he enjoyed being with Peaches, and in all honesty he felt she was better suited for his lifestyle as a hustler, Javon still had the same aspirations as any other hard-working member of society. The rules were the same no matter what: you fuck the freaks, but you marry the queens. Fatima was a queen, no doubt about it.

"Okay, we can go," Fatima announced, walking back to where Javon stood. "If they need me, they'll call me on my cell."

It was a breezy Manhattan day. A chill hung on the air, reminding everyone of the coming winter. Fatima and Javon, bundled up in their jackets, made their way through the semi-crowded sidewalk, stopping at a corner cafe on 46th street. They found a private little table near the back and ordered some hot chocolate.

"Okay, boss, what's the deal?" Fatima joked.

"Well, first of all, I want you to know that Craig, Charles and I all believe in you. We know you have what it takes to make it big."

"Thank you."

"You're welcome, but also understand that a lot of this business is about judging a book by the cover. A lot of times, style is just as important, and sometimes, it seems more important than substance …"

"I know where this is going," Fatima interrupted.

"You do?" Javon was puzzled.

"Sure, the old 'sex sells' speech. You want me to use some sex appeal to help push my CD. Sort of like Beyonce does. I had a feeling this would come up sooner or later. It always does."

"Does it now?" Javon played along.

"Yeah, but I look at it like this. Beyonce plays up her sexiness because her songs are lousy."

"That sounds like you got a little hate in your blood." Javon smiled.

"Nah, I'm not hating on the sista. To be honest, I think she can sing, but her songs are lousy bubblegum selections. My songs are saying something. Javon, we don't have to peddle flesh to push my music. Give it a chance and you'll see," she argued.

"Okay, but before you get hysterical, that's not what I wanted to talk to you about."

"It wasn't? So, why did you let me make a fool out of myself?" Fatima was slightly embarrassed by her little spiel.

"You weren't making a fool of yourself. Your argument made good sense. Besides, you were just too cute to stop."

As soon as he said it, he wished he hadn't. He didn't want to cross that line into something neither of them was ready for. Fortunately, Fatima let the line fly as if she hadn't heard it.

"Let me get to the business at hand. Craig is worried about your connection to the Nubian Temple. The atmosphere is crazy right now. The war in Iraq, the threats from Al-Qaeda; people are afraid of anyone too radical, and those people at the Temple have been rumored to be involved in some pretty radical stuff. Not to mention that your father adds another dimension to it altogether."

"My father?" Fatima was angered. "What does my father have to do with any of this?" she challenged him.

"Fatima, your father is Kareem Amir! He's…"

"I know who my father is," Fatima interrupted him. "What have you been doing, checking up on me?"

"No one is checking up on you. It's not like that."

"Then what is it like? Why is my father the topic of discussion?"

Javon didn't want to argue with her, but her attitude was beginning to upset him. He hadn't said anything negative about her father. He respected her father, but she was in a business where the media loved controversy. Did she really think her father being one of the most well known black revolutionaries next to Malcolm X wasn't going to mean something?

"Fatima, this isn't about your father. I have a great deal of respect for your father. But the bottom line is, you will soon be in the eye of the media, and don't think they're going to ignore the fact that you are Kareem Amir's daughter. You may have people who will campaign against you just for that reason alone."

"So, what am I supposed to do? Stop going to the Temple? Lie about who my father is? What is it that you and Mr. Thomas want me to do?"

"Whatever you do is up to you, but you need to remember that the work that you and those who are riding with you on this project are doing, depends on whatever you decide to do. I know it's not fair to put that on you, but that's the way things are."

"Yeah, isn't that always the case?"

Fatima wasn't really angry with Javon, but he was there and at the moment she needed to vent.

"Listen, I don't know what you expect, but my father is who he is and I'm his daughter. I'm not ashamed of either of us, and I'm not going to hide who I am or what I believe in. My job is to sing the songs the best I can, and I'm doing that. It's your job to sell them. Maybe you and Mr. Thomas should concentrate more on taking care of that responsibility and spend a little less time digging into my past."

Fatima stood and hurried out of the cafe, leaving Javon speechless at the table.

Triple Crown Publications presents . . .

TWENTY-NINE | "Fatima, what happened?"

Aaliyah was stunned by Fatima's revelation that she might have to look for another label. "I thought you told me you could trust these guys."

"It's not really that, 'Liyah. It's more about me just having the opportunity to be me," Fatima explained.

She was sitting Indian style on the floor, between Aaliyah's legs. Aaliyah sat on the sofa, grooming Fatima's locks and oiling her scalp.

"What's that supposed to mean? Did they ask you to change your style or something?"

"Not really, but they found out about Baba, and they're worried the public might not support me."

"Tima, your daddy was a hero. Black people love him."

"Well, they don't seem to think so."

Fatima never viewed her Baba as anyone other than a loving father. Of course, growing up, she knew that people in her village looked up to her father. Villagers would often tell her, "Daughter, your father is a great man loved by many in our village." But it made perfect sense to her that they would say so, since he made life so much easier for her and the villagers. Both Baba and Mama Salamah were essential to the village she grew up in.

It was only when she came to the United States that she truly learned the extent of her father's struggles. As she learned of her father's trials and tribulations, for the sake of his people, she began to look at him in a different light. She would often cry in her bed at night, partly out of pride, and partly from empathy. Many countless nights, she lay awake at night, wondering what her own life had in store for her.

Two things she had learned quickly in America. First, that she was no longer just Fatima. She was the daughter of Kareem Amir, and that came with expectations, both good and bad. The other thing she learned was that in America, there was no ambivalence. You had those who loved and praised her father, and those who hated him. Those sentiments usually ran along color lines. As Aaliyah had stated, for the most part, black people loved her father, just as they loved Malcolm, and as they loved Assata. Whites, on the other hand, in a large majority, feared and hated him.

Over the years, Fatima became defensive whenever her father was mentioned. The idea that she was being persecuted for being the daughter of a man she loved and admired angered her more than she wanted to admit. The fact that Javon was part of the cabal pitted against her father felt like a betrayal.

"They also think that I shouldn't be seen at the Temple," she informed Aaliyah.

"What?" Aaliyah was shocked. "They can't be serious."

"Yeah, they are. They say the people at the Temple are too radical."

"You know what? I'm tired of people always talking about things they know nothing about. Just because we're not brainwashed like the rest of these tap dancing Negroes, we got to be some crazy radicals." Aaliyah was getting flustered. The Temple was one of the most important things in her life.

"I know."

"It just ain't fair, Tima. Every time black people get some backbone, we got to worry about what white folks think. I'm tired of that crap. We haven't done anything wrong, anything we should

be ashamed of, or anything we need to apologize for. And I'm surprised at that cute one who came to the Temple that day. He was
there, Tima, he knows. I saw it in his face when he was listening
to Baba Askari's sermon. You know what Tima, you should go to
a different label. It would serve them right when you blow up big
without them."

"But what if they're right? What if I end up hurting my
career?" Aaliyah could see the turmoil that Fatima was in. Aaliyah
knew that the Temple was just as important to Fatima as it was to
her, but she also knew that all her life, Fatima wanted to sing. Her
loyalties were tearing her apart.

"Tima, that's not going to happen. Nobody can sing like you.
If anyone was ever meant to be a star, it's you. Trust in your
music."

Years ago, when Fatima was in the hospital after her suicide
attempt, singing was the last thing on her mind. She had had let
go of the dream of ever being a singer. Aaliyah, who was a young
volunteer nurse at the time, would stop by Fatima's room everyday to talk to her. She would sneak magazines or junk food to her.
It was during one of these covert girl gossip sessions that Aaliyah
found out that Fatima could sing. They had been discussing Chris
Baylor's latest hit, when Fatima let it slip that she used to sing
background for him. From that moment on Aaliyah would beg
Fatima to sing to her. Though Fatima and Aaliyah had become
good friends, Fatima continuously refused.

When she was released from the hospital, Fatima and Aaliyah
continued to befriend one another. It was Aaliyah who first
brought Fatima to the Temple, and who first introduced her to
Solomon. He was two years older than Fatima, but she felt like he
was ten years wiser. The more she came to know him, the more
she realized what an enigma he was to her. He was intelligent and
well-read. He could easily hold his own in a political conversation
or in any debate of sophistication. Yet, he was by his own viola-

tion, a street soldier. He loved the lure of the outlaw life.

Fatima and Solomon soon became an item, but even more, they became each other's obsession. She was trying to save him from a life of reckless pursuits that could only end in tragedy, and he was trying to mend her heart that had been shattered into a million pieces.

The first time Fatima' s voice carried a tune again, it was for Solomon. She sang for him as they lay in each other's arms after a night of passion. It was he who pushed her back to the one joy her heart knew, and it was he who taught her to be strong. Together, they made a pact. She would pursue her dream of singing and he would put the gun down and turn away from crime. Together, they would overcome every obstacle and make their own fairy tale ending. It was their destiny. Fatima recalled that now. She pulled it out of her memory and held on to it.

"Aaliyah, you' re right. It is my destiny and I'm not going to let anyone change that. I'm going to stay at the label as I am. They can either accept it or let me go. But I'm not going to compromise my dream for anyone!"

"So be it!" Aaliyah agreed.

THIRTY | Javon walked into his office and closed the

door. He had to admit, when Craig came to him with the proposal to build this label, he saw it as a way to make his money legit. Also, to put some distance between himself and his hustle. It wasn't that Javon feared running the streets. He had been pushing drugs for years now, and though he did not always agree that violence was the best way to handle every situation, he was smart enough to understand that it couldn't be avoided. So, from time to time, he had put his work in, and just accepted it as part of the game.

What really bothered Javon was that he wanted more than just the streets. His mother and Raheem had always motivated him to do something with his life. He couldn't even count the lectures he had heard from them about not becoming another black man running the streets with no direction and no future. That was one of the reasons he went to college. Yet in spite of all that, he had become exactly what he sought to avoid.

Ironically, that was the thing about being black in America. The economics of the ghetto confronted you all the time. Of course, it didn't mean you had to turn to crime, and he didn't want to be one of those people who used the ghetto for an excuse. Still, he knew the dynamics of the ghetto made it more probable that you would turn to crime, and that's what black people faced. It only took so much struggling to make ends meet on a nine to five before that bootleg CD or DVD began to look like a better buy than the one from the store. Or the $800 coat you get from Lisa for $250, although you knew she probably boosted it. Before long, you start to justify it. It's not illegal to take advantage of a bargain. You know, make that hard earned buck stretch a little further. But with each step, each little bargain, the line between crime and innocence begins to blur, until $1,000 to drop a package off at an address across town doesn't sound bad.

The fact is, every ghetto in America has a thriving economic base grounded in crime, and when you have a bunch of people living from check to check, with only two dollars above rent money to their name, it's more probable than not that they will follow the money trail to crime. Because after everything is said and done, money talks and bullshit walks. That's the American dream in its rawest form.

Javon couldn't help thinking that his life should have been different, and now, through this music label, it was happening. That thought alone inspired him.

Craig was scheduled for a late afternoon meeting to negotiate G-Rydah going on tour with M.O.P. and Fat Joe. He had asked Javon to attend. But it was still only noon, and Javon had nothing to do. He was considering driving down to Fatima' s video shoot to see her. They had finally gotten past the little outburst in the cafe a few weeks ago. To her credit, Fatima had stood her ground. She would not let Craig or Javon convince her to turn her back on what she held in her heart. Craig didn't like it, but Javon, though not saying so, approved.

He always found it funny how quickly they had really clicked. Sure, she looked good enough to catch any man's eye, but it was more than that. She had that something special that made her stand out. There was no way you could be around her and mistake her for the average woman. Javon had her on his mind when the intercom disrupted him.

"Mr. Williams, you have a Ms. Patricia Wells here to see you."

His secretary's announcement brought a sigh of irritation from Javon.

"Show her in, Ms. Jones," Javon replied.

He let go of the intercom button and a few seconds later, Peaches was walking through the door.

"What are you doing here?" Javon asked, getting up from behind his desk to lock the door.

"Damn, what kind of welcome is that?"

"It's just that I wasn't expecting you."

"Well, I wanted to see your office ... besides, I was in the city and figured I'd take you to lunch, if you're free."

Peaches walked around checking out Javon's office. She was impressed and a little jealous. His office in the back of his club was one thing, but an expensive office in a Midtown high-rise was big time. Peaches felt awkward, like she was out of her element, and she didn't like the feeling. In the back of her mind, she couldn't help thinking that Javon was trying to be something he wasn't, and it didn't sit right with her.

"Peaches, I was getting ready to check out a video shoot."

Javon wasn't in the mood for Peaches' company right now. He hadn't seen her in weeks and whenever he did see her she was always begging to get on the hottest party's V.I.P. list, and that started to annoy the hell out of him. Besides, he'd grown past the point of being able to freak a stripper at free well.

Javon sat on the edge of his desk. Peaches walked over and slipped between his legs.

"Can I go with you?" she asked.

"They don't want people at the shoot hanging out." He hunched his shoulders.

"Who says it's just to hang out?"

"Not today, okay?" He shook his head. "I'll take you another time."

Peaches, upset with Javon's answer, flopped down in a leather seat facing his desk.

"Javon, you know I can dance, and I look as good as any of those video girls. When are you going to plug me in?" She reached in her bag.

"Peaches, I told you before, I don't pick the girls for the videos," Javon replied, trying to keep his composure.

"Yeah, but you can still put a word in for me. Or what is it? You don't want to see nobody else come up?"

Peaches was frustrated with Javon. She knew he had to have some say around there. At the least he could set her up with an introduction to the director. She knew once they saw her they would give her a try. But ever since Javon got serious about this music shit, he was acting like he was too good for her, and that shit was starting to irk her.

She dug around her bag and pulled out some weed and a blunt. Yet, before she could begin rolling it up, Javon spoke up. "Don't start rolling weed in this office," he admonished.

"I know you ain't serious." She cocked her head to the side. "The door is locked. Ain't no one going to walk in here."

"That's not the point. This is a place of business. You should always be professional, you need to learn that."

"Nigga, please, you got an office in Midtown and now you're Mr. Got to act professional. Ain't it funny how fast a nigga change," Peaches retorted sarcastically.

The statement angered Javon. What Peaches failed to realize was that succeeding in business was about being professional. How you carried yourself under certain circumstances made the difference between success and failure. Anyway, it didn't matter, because Javon had no intention of taking time to explain his actions to her. As far as he was concerned, Peaches was one of those aspects of his street life that he was keeping separate from this one.

"It's time for you to go." Javon reached down, grabbing

Peaches by the arm.

"Come on, baby, I was just playing."

"I got work to do. I'll get with you later." He pointed to door. "Bye."

Peaches got up, grabbing her bag with attitude and making her way to the door.

"Fuck you, Javon!" she spat. "You ain't about shit, nigga!" She stormed out, slamming the door behind her.

Javon shook his head in disappointment, realizing probably for the first time that he was going to have to let her go before she became more of a headache.

Triple Crown Publications presents . . .

THIRTY-ONE | Utica Ave. crossed Atlantic Ave., ran

past the track field, then curved into Fulton Street. This was on one side of Boys and Girls High School. Derrick watched the high school kids letting out as he waited for the light to turn. Boys and Girls High School had always been a trouble spot, not that violence in school was limited to this one locale. Thomas Jefferson, Pacific, Redirection, and Sterling, were among the trouble schools in Brooklyn.

As he drove past, Derrick took in the jostling and posturing of these young ghetto soldiers parading by in their street uniforms: sagging jeans and Timberland boots. The streets were its own rites of passage, and by this time, these young warriors had already seen too many rough times to believe that the rest of their lives would be anything else but more of the same pain and suffering. Their journey into manhood came with the hard reality that with each day came another struggle. Derrick knew that in spite of his own trials in life, he had been blessed. While many turned to the streets looking for a way to survive, he had been born and raised into the hustlin' lifestyle.

By the age of nine, he was sitting at the kitchen table, helping the matriarch of the family bag up twenties of coke and dimes of dope. Highly valued pearls of wisdom had been fed to him directly from the mouth of Big Stan, one of the East Coast's most notorious hustlers, simply because he was also Derrick's father. Of course, the death of Big Stan had been one of the most well-learned lessons his father had ever taught him. Simply put, no matter who you were, if you used drugs, you were just another fiend who was one bad shot away from the morgue.

Derrick drove down Fulton Street, made a left on Ralph Ave., and parked across from the Brevort projects. He had made a weekly visit to this house for the last three years. Across the street from the projects, half way down the block of Macon Street, was the three-story brownstone Derrick made his way to.

Derrick pushed open the metal gate that separated the concrete front yard from the concrete sidewalk. Derrick always found the lack of grass disturbing. New York really was a concrete jungle; even the front yard bore witness to this unnatural state.

As Derrick was about to ring the bell, he heard the excited shrieks of the little girl, who happened to be barreling her way toward him.

"Uncle Derrick! Uncle Derrick!" Derrick turned and bent to catch the small bundle coming at him, then scooped her up and held her in his arms.

"Hey, there, princess. Ain't you getting big?" he playfully addressed her. "What you doing out here by yourself?"

"Me and Trevor are playing." Trevor was the older of the two children. He was nine, which made him two years older than Chantel, the little girl that now occupied Derrick's arms.

"Well, where is your brother?" Derrick asked.

"He's down the block with the other kids."

"Is your mommy here?" Derrick asked, finally setting her down.

"Yeah," she replied, and then took off, pushing open the front door, and yelling as she ran inside. "Mommy, Mommy, Uncle Derrick is here!"

Derrick followed her in. His niece and nephew were the only relatives he had in New York. It always gave him a little peace of mind to spend time with them.

"Girl, stop running in the house, acting like you crazy or something," Felicia's voice shouted out from the kitchen.

As Derrick entered that part of the house, he found Felicia wiping her hands on a dishrag. She took Chantal by the shoulder and turned her toward the door.

"Go get your brother and both of you get cleaned up so we can eat," Felicia instructed her daughter. Chantal once again took off running past Derrick. "And stop running!" Felicia yelled after her.

"What are you cooking?" Derrick asked, flopping down on one of the stools in Felicia's kitchen.

"Boy, whatever I'm cooking, you going to eat it anyway, so it don't make a bit of difference, now do it?" Felicia turned back to tending the pots she had on the stove.

Derrick liked Felicia. They had an easy friendship. Ironically, it hadn't always been like that. In 1996, Felicia had a two-year-old son by Derrick's older brother Erick. She was also pregnant with Chantal and convinced that she and Erick were going to live happily ever after, as husband and wife. Then the Feds came and snatched Erick up, carting him away to MCC, the federal detention center in Manhattan. It was during one of her visits to see Erick at MCC that Felicia bumped into Erick's wife. Yes, Erick was married, and had three children by the woman. For three years, Felicia had unknowingly been the other woman. Embarrassed, pregnant and angry, Felicia disappeared.

When Derrick returned from the military, Erick asked Derrick to track her down. It took three years before Derrick located her. It wasn't only that Erick was his brother that motivated him. Derrick just didn't agree with a woman keeping a child away from the father. Often, if a man went to prison, the mother of his children would refuse to take the children to see him. Whatever the dispute, Derrick believed a man had the right to connect with his children. Derrick had no intention of letting Felicia rob his brother of that right.

The first day he had stopped at Felicia's door, he had been determined he would either convince her with words or with brute force. Surprisingly, Felicia was not against the idea of Erick seeing his children. She agreed to the visitation, as long as someone she trusted would accompany them. She refused, however, to ever deal with Erick herself.

Derrick understood her anger and respected her wishes. More than that, Derrick respected her. In the three years since she disappeared, she had finished school and landed a corporate job on Wall Street. She had put a down payment on the brownstone she was now living in, and was taking good care of the children on her own. What really gained Derrick's respect was information he gained during Erick's appeal. Erick's lawyer learned that the Feds had threatened Felicia with prosecution and the loss of her children if she didn't offer information against Erick and his family. This had been the real reason for her disappearance, and why she had not resurfaced until after Erick's conviction.

Knowing that Felicia was a stand-up type of woman had caused Derrick to look at her in a different light. That was when he started dropping in on them to make sure that she and the kids were always all right. Felicia hardly ever accepted money from Derrick, although Derrick would buy things for her and the kids. Still, he did what he could, and what she would allow.

"How's Erick?" Felicia casually asked.

"He's surviving. Trying to make the best out of a bad situation."

"Ain't we all," she stated. She turned the heat down on the stove and went to set the table.

"He'd love to see you." Derrick watched for her response.

"That's not going to happen, Derrick, so we don't even have to go there."

It wasn't said with bitterness, but with resolve. Derrick

changed the subject. "How's work?"

"I'm doing good. Thinking about striking out on my own."

"Oh yeah?" Derrick was impressed.

"Yeah, I know the market is kind of bad right now, but I've established a good reputation as a financial advisor. The bills are paid up, including the house, and I got a little something put away in the bank. So I can rough it out until I start earning like what I want."

"Well, you know I got your back if you need some help," Derrick informed her.

"Yeah, I know, but I can't accept your help. Especially for this."

"Why not?"

"Derrick, the last thing I need is the Feds taking everything I worked so hard to build."

"You're exaggerating. The Feds ain't looking for you."

"You're right, and I want to keep it like that. I read about that girl Kemba Smith, so I know I don't have to be selling drugs; all I have to be is tied to drug dealers, and my ass could be in prison, too. Trevor and Chantal already tie me to y'all."

"So, now my family is dragging you down?" Derrick responded, slightly annoyed.

"Boy, I didn't say that, so stop putting words in my mouth."

"But that's what you meant."

"You don't know what I'm thinking, so stop trying to tell me what I mean. I said what I meant."

"You've never wanted to take money from the family and you got far away from us after Derrick got arrested."

"Stop right there, Derrick. I was there for your brother. He wasn't there for me. He's the one who had a family I didn't know about. So don't try to blame that on me. And yeah, you're right, I don't want money from your family. Not because I don't love them, but because I love myself and my kids too much to put us

169

at risk. Derrick, you lost your whole family because of their involvement in drugs, and look at you. You still neck-deep in the same shit. As smart as you are, you're playing a stupid game that will have you in the same boat they're in. So please excuse me if I choose not to go along for the ride."

"You're wrong about that one, Felicia... I won't be going to prison."

"Yeah, you got a plan on beating the system. Don't kid yourself, Derrick. You ain't the first and probably won't be the last that held that same thought."

"I'm also not—" Trevor and Chantal came running in before Derrick could finish his sentence.

"What's up, Uncle Dee?" Trevor approached Derrick.

He was only nine, but already had the street-smart swagger that said the boy was headed for trouble. The age of innocence was diminishing with every generation. It's no longer unheard of to see a ten-year-old with access to a gun or a girl of thirteen already sexually active. New York streets were full of gangs; most of them teens. He wondered if Trevor was already involved in one.

"What's up, little homie? What you been up to?"

"I'm chilling. We're going to see Daddy next week. You going with us?"

"I don't know, we'll see."

"Come on, you know it's time to eat," Felicia announced, shooing the kids toward the table. The kids made their way to the table. Derrick also found his spot, and sat down to eat with his family.

The rest of the conversation was light banter, the kind that fits right at home in a close knit family. But in spite of the good atmosphere, Derrick found himself concerned. He knew Felicia was a strong woman. She had proven that time and again in all that she had accomplished for herself. But that was exactly what nagged at Derrick. She was by herself. She was a single black mother, with two kids to raise, in a drug infested, crime-ridden ghetto. The odds were against her. Derrick wasn't going to count her out; he had faith in her, but he couldn't help wondering how long before the monstrosity of it all came barreling through the door of this happy home.

Triple Crown Publications presents . . .

THIRTY-TWO | Javon and Craig were backstage at the Apollo, Harlem's most well known venue. Craig had been on his cell phone and two-way for hours, trying to contact G-Rydah. Their partner, Charles Jackson, had gotten G-Rydah added to the Harlem Nights AIDS Benefit. He had been scheduled to perform and should have arrived at least an hour ago. Craig was pacing backstage, fuming that he couldn't reach G-Rydah, his assistant or the bodyguard. All of whom should have been together. Craig wasn't sure if this was more of G-Rydah's increasingly annoying antics or if something had seriously happened, and the uncertainty was what frustrated him.

"What's the word?" Javon asked.

Craig raised his hand, signaling for Javon to wait, as he continued to talk into his cell phone. Finishing his conversation, he ended the call and turned to face Javon.

"They should have been here. They left two hours ago," Craig explained.

"So where the fuck are they?" Javon asked.

"I don't know, but I got a feeling that—"

Before Craig could finish the sentence, his cell phone rang. He answered it, while Javon pondered the situation. G-Rydah had already developed a strong fan base. Missing this show wouldn't affect his sales, but it would complicate his relationship with the benefit promoters and some of the other industry big wigs that were behind the show. It was never a good idea to let down record executives, they had away of holding grudges forever.

"They got arrested."

"What?!" Javon responded, stunned at the news.

"They got arrested," he repeated, putting his phone away. "That was Charles, they're in the precinct. It had something to do with drugs in the car." Craig explained.

"You're kidding!"

"I wish I was. Charles is taking care of it. He'll keep us posted." Craig shook his head in exasperation. "I don't know how much more of this Charles is going to be willing to put up with."

"What about the show?"

"They won't be out in time to make it. You know how slow the process is. They'll be really lucky if they get out by tomorrow."

"Damn."

"Yeah, damn is right. That boy is becoming a headache. Now we got to tell the coordinator that he won't be performing and that's going to be a mark against us. That's not the way to build a solid career in this business."

"What if we substitute Fatima? She's in the audience. We can get her to perform in his place."

"She didn't come ready to perform. Her back up singers ain't here and she didn't bring any music with her."

"Well, let's at least ask her and see what she can come up with. That way we'll still have someone out there representing the label."

"Okay," Craig agreed. "First, let's talk to her, and then I'll try and fix it up with the benefit coordinator and the stage show's director."

Twenty minutes later, Fatima was backstage trying to figure out a performance.

"Okay, Fatima, we got the guitar, and the keyboard man from Chole's band said he'd back you up, since they already performed. You ready to do your thing?" Craig asked.

He was once again feeling invigorated. Fatima was just as good a performer as G-Rydah, and an even better choice right now, because the exposure would help promote her.

"Yeah, I'm ready," she replied. Craig wished he had more time to better set her up for the performance, but on the spur of the moment, he had done the best he could. The rest was up to her. He had confidence in her ability.

The emcee came to the wings and asked, "Y'all ready?"

"Yeah, we're ready," Craig replied. The emcee nodded and made his way back to the stage. "This is your house tonight, Fatima, show them what you're made of," Craig encouraged Fatima.

Javon walked up to Fatima and took her hand. Fatima looked into his face, but he didn't say anything. He didn't have to. He gently squeezed her hand and gave her a slight nod. Fatima nodded back. She understood. Tonight wasn't just about her. Tonight she was repping for the label.

"I won't let y'all down."

With those last words she made her way to the stage.

"She's going to do all right," Craig said, more in thought to himself then in conversation, but Javon answered anyway.

"I know."

"I spoke with Charles; he said it was the same cop who arrested G-Rydah and the rest of the crew."

"Sergeant Canelli?" Javon inquired.

"Yeah, he pulled G-Rydah's SUV over to search it. Someone had some weed on them and decided to stuff it in between the seats. The cop found it and took everyone in for it."

"What's the deal with this cop anyway? Why does he keep stopping our people?"

"Money. What else? He's trying to squeeze us for a salary," Craig answered, disgusted with the whole situation.

"What are you talking about?"

"Every time one of these rappers start making it big, New York's finest come around offering the services of off duty cops for security. One of the perks to hiring them is you don't get pulled over. If you got a badge in the car with you, you get a free pass."

"And if you don't hire them?" Javon asked.

"Well, if you don't hire them, they make it their business to let you know they're around. They probably got G-Rydah's ride on their shit list."

"So what are we going to do about it?"

"Nothing we can do, it's part of the business. On the West Coast, you got to pay the gangs. On the East Coast, the police are the gangs. Either way, you got to pay someone."

"I don't like the idea of us getting squeezed, no matter who it is." Javon was angered by Craig's apathy.

"It's the same as G-Rydah's entourage of thugs. He's taking care of them and they don't do anything but cause problems everywhere they go. He might as well put one of them cops on the payroll now and keep them off our backs."

"It's not the same. Those thugs, as you call them, are his homies. They were there when he didn't have anything but dreams, and they'll probably be there if he fell tomorrow. Those cops, on the other hand, don't give a fuck about him. They're just pressing him 'cause he got money. They hate to see a nigga on the come up, but they're quick to have their hands out."

"Don't let it bother you, believe me, we're not the only ones in this predicament. Like I said, we hire one of them on an on and off basis, and they'll back up."

"Fuck them. We don't have to give those grimy assholes a coin."

"That's not a smart move, Javon, especially since G-Rydah and his homies have a habit of driving around with drugs and guns in their cars. We don't need them getting locked up every other week."

The emcee was announcing Fatima on stage.

"Let me work it out," Javon replied, making his way toward the stage.

Craig followed, thinking that this time, Javon's help might be more problematic than just going with the flow. If Craig knew anything about this business, it was that some battles weren't worth fighting. Any further thoughts got lost in the roar of the crowd. New York's tough crowd was showing its love for the newest rising star on the horizon. She had something special. Craig smiled and looked toward Javon, finding him likewise entranced.

As the crowd quieted down, Fatima began playing her guitar, and the keyboard merged with her tune. Then, from nowhere, that unbelievable voice took control. The rest, they say, was musical history.

Triple Crown Publications presents . . .

THIRTY-THREE | Fatima stood on the balcony of

her hotel suite overlooking Hollywood. Tinsel Town shone full of glitter, brightly lit against the dark night, a beacon of hope to believers. Fatima was a believer. Her soul-stirring performance at the Apollo a month ago had received rave reviews. It brought on an onslaught of media attention and dozens of invitations by the rich and famous. Those who were smart enough to smell fame and fortune in the air for Fatima. It was clear to everyone that the fickle world of fans and media gods had chosen her as their newest rising star.

As far back as Fatima could remember, she had wanted nothing less than to sing, and for her music to touch other people. Now on the brink of stardom, she felt redeemed. For all she had suffered she was going to be a star. Silent tears of joy escaped her eyes as she surveyed the worlds beyond her balcony. Her serene moment of reflection was interrupted by a gentle knock on the door.

"Yes?" she inquired, reluctantly letting go of the moment.

"Fatima, it's me. Are you ready for dinner?" Javon's voice carried through the adjoining door to the suite.

"Yeah, come in."

She quickly wiped the tears from her eyes, and after taking a few more seconds to compose herself and one final glance into the world of make-believe, she turned around to face Javon. He was standing just inside her room, looking good as usual. She couldn't deny the emotions he awakened in her. The months of working with him close by had evolved into a comfortable familiarity between them. Yet it was underlined with a clear attraction. Feeling giddy and elated, she walked toward him and surprised him with a playful kiss on the cheek.

"What was that for?" Javon asked, looking in her eyes. He saw they were moist, and he had the feeling she had been crying.

"Just because."

She smiled and it warmed his heart.

"Are you okay?" he asked.

"Yeah...finally."

Javon looked deep into her eyes. He was caught in their gleam, lost in their eternity. Her smile slowly faded. There was a silence between them that spoke volumes. Dancing in his eyes, Fatima found a myriad of possibilities. It excited her. Raised the hair on the back of her neck and caused goose bumps to rise on her flushed skin.

She stood transfixed as his hands reached up to cradle her face, and then they kissed again. This time the kiss was intimate, passionately acknowledging that something, that until this moment, they had both been avoiding. It was at the moment that she knew, they both knew, there would be no turning back.

No words were needed. His strong embrace, her tender touch, it all took on a life it's own. A natural choreography of longing and fulfillment played out with each movement. Javon commandingly traced her feminine form. His hands finding her supple breasts cupping them and feeling their nipples grow taut, even through the fabric of her blouse. A slight moan escaped Fatima' s lips as she felt her heart beating excitedly within her chest.

Javon kissed her again, drawing her body into his. She could feel his excitement and responded by sensually rubbing her body against his. Javon pulled back from her long enough to question the moment. Though he wanted her, he had to make sure it's what she wanted, too.

"Do you want this, Fatima?"

She responded with a nod, already engrossed in the thralls of desire.

And so their dance began. Javon unbuttoned her blouse, exposing her sable skin. Then gently, he placed tender kisses on the flesh of her heaving chest. Reaching down, he loosened her pants and let them fall. The dark hue of her body stood in delicious contrast to the light color of her undergarments. Javon reached around her, releasing her beautiful breasts from their lace confines. He moistened a fingertip with his mouth, then traced her chocolate brown areolas, before taking her breast into his mouth.

His free hand roamed down her flat belly, finding her panty line and going beyond it in search of her core. Fatima's acquiescence was found in the slight movement by which she further parted her legs. His fingers found her wet and inviting. She responded, first with another moan lower and more intense than the first, and the next by reaching for the front of his pants and massaging his growing manhood.

For the briefest moment, her thoughts went to Solomon. She was flooded with guilt, but the expertise of Javon's fingers wiped away those thoughts, leaving in its stead a ravenous lust that needed to be satisfied.

Knowing what her body craved, Javon scooped her up, and carried her to the bedroom. Laying her down on the edge of the bed, he pulled her panties off. She was a dark beauty. Javon lowered his head to her warm, moist center and feasted on her essence. He took his time. Using his mouth and his fingers, he expertly brought her to ecstasy, time and time again.

When Javon had Fatima so sensitive that his slightest touch could drown her in pleasure, he stripped his clothes off and holding her hips firmly, entered her. With powerful stroke after stroke,

Javon brought Fatima over the edge. Delight washed over her as her body trembled with pleasure. Only then did Javon, himself, release and achieve his pleasure. He watched Fatima. She was in that special place where bliss is all that exists. Feeling good Javon kissed her softly on the side of the neck.

After an hour of sleeping and being wrapped in each other's embrace, Javon woke up and began caressing the side of Fatima's face. His fingertips seemed to be melting into her soft skin as she started to mumble.

"What you say, baby?" Javon asked.

"Uhmm," Fatima said, groggily. "I love you, Solomon. I really do."

THIRTY-FOUR | Peaches stepped out of the club

exhausted. It was one of those nights when every trick in the city wanted to feel her up. Usually, she didn't give a fuck. She had grown accustomed to the gropes and pawing she experienced. As long as a nigga realized it wasn't for free, it was all gravy. Tonight, though, she was distracted. Her thoughts were on Javon.

Earlier, she had been in the dressing room getting ready to hit the floor, when Sandra came waltzing in with that damn *Source* magazine. She had flipped it open and dropped it on the table in front of Peaches.

"Yo, girl, check out your man."

There it was, a picture of Javon at some industry party, hugged up with that new R&B singer, Fatima. Peaches was upset but decided to play it cool and not show her frustration.

"That ain't about nothing." She tossed the magazine at Sandra. "That's just one of the artists on his label."

"Well, I don't know about you, but I wouldn't be letting no bitch, artist or not, get all up under my man like that."

"I ain't sweating that. Besides, that nigga knows he got a good thing; he ain't about to fuck that up."

"Peaches, be for real. I ain't met a nigga yet who turns down some pussy when it's thrown at him. And from this picture, it damn sure looks like honey is throwing it at Javon."

"Girl, you know ain't no fake-ass India Arie look alike got a chance fucking with me. That nigga ain't going to play himself for no half-ass bitch like that. Sandra, that nigga sprung on this pussy; he ain't going nowhere."

"I hear you, Ms. Thang. That's your cock, so you call the shot. I'm just putting you on so you don't be in the blind, feel me?"

"Yeah, yeah, I feel you, but sweetie, I got it all under control," Peaches assured Sandra.

The rest of the night, Peaches worked the floor and made her money, but her mind was on Javon. What was that nigga thinking? For weeks now, he had been claiming to be busy every time she wanted to hang out. Peaches was about that cheddar, so she understood business was business, but she wasn't even profiting from all this shit and that, more than anything, had her vexed.

She had asked Javon a couple of times to put in a word for her with one of the video directors and he had refused each time. Now, the nigga was all up in a magazine hugged up with some lame-ass broad. Peaches wasn't stupid. Not by a long shot. She realized things weren't going her way. She had to find a way to use Javon's influence to set herself up and she had to do it quick.

"Peaches, where you parked at?" Sandra asked.

"Oh, I'm right down the block."

"Want me to get Rory to walk you?"

"Nah, I'm straight. I'll see you tomorrow."

Peaches walked toward her car. She was thinking about stepping her game up. The nigga Javon was playing games. She might just have to holla at that young boy, G-Rydah. She knew he was one of the artists Javon had been working with. If she went to the next label party, she could find a way to get the little nigga alone for a minute and get him to agree to put her in one of his videos. Peaches smiled at the thought. If Javon kept fucking up, she might even give the little nigga some pussy. Bet Javon won't think he's so fucking cute then.

Peaches reached her car, turned the alarm off and put the key in the door. Just as she opened the door, she sensed a presence behind her. She had been so lost in thought that she hadn't noticed before. As she started to turn to see who it was, she felt an arm wrapping around her neck and pulling her backwards. The sudden violence of the attack threw her off balance. She fought to regain her footing, but slipped.

"Give me the fucking key, bitch," a harsh voice boomed at her. It was then that she saw the glint of the knife flash before her eyes, and a terror took hold.

"I said give me the fucking key. Don't make me cut your fucking heart out, bitch," the voice boomed again, even harsher than before.

Peaches dropped the keys. Quickly, another attacker swooped in, and, picking up the keys, jumped in Peaches' Accura.

It was then that the second attacker noticed who she was. "Yo, dawg, that's that stripper bitch!" he exclaimed excitedly. "Let's throw her in the backseat and take her with us!" he continued.

The terror Peaches felt escalated with those words.

"Hell no, nigga! Fuck this bitch, we got the car, we good with that!" the first attacker responded.

"Come on, dawg, we can have some fun with her."

"Nigga, fuck this stank-ass hoe." He flung Peaches to the ground.

"But if she's a stripper, that means she's got to have some paper on her." the first attacker pressed, and started searching Peaches, as she lay out on the pavement. He took what money he could find on her.

At that moment voices could be heard coming down the block. Her attacker turned to see who was coming.

Peaches realized this might be her only opportunity to get out of this alive, and began to scream out with desperation in her voice.

"HELP! HELP ME, PLEASE!"

Before she could utter another word she was kicked in the

face. The force of the kick dazed her.

"You do that one more time and I will cut your throat," the first attacker threatened. But it was too late. Help had arrived, and relief flooded Peaches' soul.

"Hey, what's going on? Call Rory! Somebody call Rory!" a female voice screamed. The second attacker had already had the car started and was ready to take off.

"Let's go, homie!" the second attacker shouted, no longer interested in anything but getting away.

The first attacker, angry that Peaches' screams for help had attracted attention, began to viciously kick and stomp her again and again, taking her to the edge of consciousness. Then, he slipped into the backseat of the car as it drove off, leaving Peaches in a crumpled heap, her eyes swollen shut and her mouth busted and bloody.

"Oh, my God! It's Peaches! Somebody call an ambulance!" another female voice shouted.

Peaches vaguely heard the words. They sounded distant and foggy but familiar. She knew it was one of the girls from the club.

Before long, a number of the girls and Rory, the bouncer, were tending to Peaches, as she tried to shake off the pain she felt. After about twenty minutes, the cops and ambulance finally arrived.

All Peaches kept thinking was, *What a fucked up ending to a fucked-up day.*

THIRTY-FIVE | Javon couldn't believe it. She had

called him by some other nigga's name then had fallen asleep. He should have woken her ass up and asked who the fuck Solomon was, but he hadn't; instead, he had gotten dressed and left the room. He asked himself if it really mattered. She wasn't his girl. They had had a one-night stand; it wasn't a big deal. Yet, no matter how much he tried to convince himself of that, in his heart, he knew he was lying to himself. He had wanted more.

The hours of working alongside Fatima had given him hope that more could come from their relationship. Fatima wasn't just another girl to him, she was another world of possibilities. A leap from a life of uncertainty in the game to a life of legitimacy with a woman of substance to call his own. All these possibilities disappeared when she called him Solomon. The fact that she had another man in her life was bad enough, but that she was thinking about him while making love to Javon was too much.

Javon's thoughts were disrupted by the knock on his door. It was the door that separated his room from Fatima's, so he knew immediately who it was.

"Javon, it's Fatima. Can I come in?" Javon didn't respond. He was hoping she would think he was asleep, and leave.

"Javon, please open the door. We need to talk."

She continued to knock. Clearly, she had no intention of leaving, so he got up and made his way to the door. He stood there momentarily, with one hand on the doorknob, and the other on the lock. He was steeling himself before opening the door that stood between them.

"Why did you leave?" she asked, stepping through the door. "I woke up and you were gone." Javon didn't respond. Fatima hesitated, sensing something was wrong between them. "Javon, I know it's kind of awkward, but I needed to talk about what happened," she said, looking into his eyes.

"Go ahead, talk," he finally responded, finding it hard to hide his frustration.

"What's wrong?" Fatima asked with concern etched on her face.

"Nothing. Go ahead, what's on your mind?" He was becoming impatient.

"Well, after what happened between us, I feel we need to define where we stand..."

"What is there to define? We're two consenting adults who spent a night together. It's no big deal."

"That's how you feel?"

"Ain't that what happened?" Javon threw the question back at her.

Fatima was stunned; she thought that last night had meant more to him than that. For months, she had thought about Javon, considering the possibility of them being together. Then last night, overwhelmed by her emotions, she had allowed her feelings to take over and gave her body and soul to him. Now, he stood there, telling her it was no big deal. Embarrassment flushed over her. Tears began to well up in her eyes. She felt stupid. All these months of flirting and friendship had been just manipulation to get between her legs, and now that he had, it was no big deal. Fatima felt betrayed, and she felt used. But she was not the same scared little girl she once was. No, Fatima had survived the many hardships this life had saw fit to throw her way and she was smart enough to know what was important.

"No, you're right, it's no big deal. I just wanted to make sure we were clear about what we came out West for. We're here to take care of business and I don't want nothing to get in the way of

that. I make the music; you sell the records. We have a lot of people to see out here so let's just put last night behind us and get to work, okay?"

Having said her piece, Fatima turned and walked back into her room, closing the door between them and letting her tears wash away any silly notions of romantic evenings and happy endings.

Triple Crown Publications presents . . .

THIRTY-SIX | Peaches' face was bruised and swollen.
Her eyes were blackened and stitches decorated her lower lip, which was also swollen and disfigured. That was just her face. Her body had its own bruises to contend with. Yet, in spite of it all, Peaches knew she was lucky to be alive. Carjackings aren't usually dangerous. The thief wants the car, and as long as a person doesn't resist or act brave, the jacking is usually quick and painless.

But the guy who grabbed Peaches was a different story. He was vicious. He had intentions of harming someone, whether they resisted or not. You know, the kind of guy who got off on inflicting pain. If the girls hadn't come along when they did, there's no telling what could have happened. She could imagine the headlines, "Stripper found slain in parking lot." The thought sent shivers down her back.

At least the pain was subsiding. The doctors had given her enough painkillers to spare her any unnecessary agony. It hadn't gone, but it had been reduced to a dull throb, hanging around to remind her of the experience.

She didn't have time to worry about the pain. She was more concerned with how long they were planning to keep her in the hospital. Bad enough she was going to have to hear a million "I told you sos" from Nana, but she damn sure didn't want to run up no crazy hospital bill as well. She had some money in the stash, but she hated to go there if she didn't have to. She first thought she would get Javon to pay for it all, but she'd been trying to reach him since they admitted her yesterday and he hadn't returned any of the messages she had left. To be honest, he had been so distant toward her these last few months, she didn't know if she could count on him at all.

Her thoughts were disrupted when the hospital room door opened. In walked Sandra. If it had been a room full of men, she would have drawn every eye. She didn't have to try, the girl was simply the truth. Seeing her made Peaches feel better.

"What's up, girl?" Sandra cheerfully greeted her.

She had come from the club last night to see her but had left when the doctors had pumped Peaches full of medication to make her sleep.

"What's up, homie?" Peaches replied, words pouring through damaged lips.

"I just came to check out how ugly in the face you done got so I can go snatch up all your customers."

If anyone other than Sandra had said it, Peaches would have taken offense, but her girl was always saying shit like that. Sandra didn't care what the situation was or who felt what way about it. She said what she felt like saying, and fuck who didn't like it. Her sharp tongue had definitely sliced enough men and women.

"Girl, I could look like Shrek and you still couldn't take my customers," Peaches replied.

"Girl, you better not bet on that," Sandra laughed. She walked over to the bed, looking Peaches over. "Damn, why them faggots had to do this? They could have just took the car and bounced."

"I don't know, but I'm glad it ain't turn out worse."

"Yeah, I know what you mean. Remember Carmen?"

All the girls at the club knew about Carmen. She was the pretty Puerto Rican girl who used to work at the club. One night this guy starts tipping her big money and asking to take her home. Carmen, thinking she had herself a trick, jumps in his car. Two days later, her body was found. She had been raped, beaten, strangled and left in a garbage bin. Carmen's story became the reminder to all the girls of the dangers they faced. Not that Peaches had gone out looking for this, but she understood the connection. Life could get ugly at any moment, so if you escaped a tragedy with just a few bumps and bruises, sometimes you had to look at it as a blessing, because it could have been worse.

"Yeah, I remember, and for a minute there I thought I was going to end up just like her," Peaches admitted.

"No, sweetheart, it ain't our time yet. Shit, I still ain't find my Mr. Right, yet." Sandra laughed, then added, "Or Mrs. Right, 'cause you know this pussy of mine is not prejudiced."

"Girl, you really are crazy." Though it pained her to laugh, Peaches couldn't help it. Sandra was a trip. They spent an hour or so talking girl talk, and gossiping about everyone.

Then the door opened and Javon walked in. He saw Sandra first.

"Damn, who's that big body hottie looking so bootyliscious?" Javon joked with her.

"Pretty boy, you had your chance and you was scared of all this here," Sandra retorted sassily, with her hands on her hips. "So don't come acting like you know what to do with it now." Javon laughed and gave her a big hug. He liked Sandra. She didn't bite her tongue and he respected that.

He turned to look at Peaches. The bruises looked bad, probably more so because she was light-skinned. The injuries disturbed Javon. He wasn't one of the woman beaters, though he knew Peaches could be a pain in the ass sometimes. Trying to control a woman with a swift backhand wasn't his style. He had been raised to understand that if a relationship needed violence to keep it in place, then it wasn't a relationship worth being in.

"How you doing?" he asked Peaches.

"Not good. I wasn't even sure if you were going to show up. I left you a couple of messages."

"I know; I was out of town."

"Yeah, I figured," Peaches responded sarcastically.

She was upset. For months, Javon had been neglecting her, and always the reason was business. She looked in his eyes, displaying the dissatisfaction she felt. Javon picked up on it and so did Sandra.

"Listen, girl, I'm going to bounce and let you love birds straighten out the wrinkles." She turned to Javon. "Pretty boy, you be good." With those few words, Sandra made her way to the door.

As soon as the door closed behind Sandra, Peaches began her tirade.

"Javon, you know I don't even see you anymore. It's been months since we've done anything together or just hung out. If I wasn't in the hospital, you probably wouldn't be with me now. So what's up, are you fucking that bitch or what? Keep it real with me. You all up in the magazines hugged up with her and got people looking at me like I'm a fool or something."

"Peaches, I'm taking care of business. Why you acting all crazy?"

"'Cause, nigga, ever since you got involved in that music shit, you done changed. You hanging around them phony-assed niggas and now everything I do you want to beef about."

"That's 'cause you ain't doing nothing but getting high and throwing tantrums when you don't get your way."

"That's bullshit! I done asked you plenty of times to plug me into one of them videos but you ain't trying to help me."

"I told you before, that ain't up to me."

"That don't mean you can't put in a word for me, Javon. You act like you want to see me fucked up in the game."

"You think it's that easy? Them girls are professional, they ain't no..."

"No what? Strippers? You embarrassed because I'm a stripper?"

"I wasn't going to say stripper."

"Then what were you going to say, huh? Nigga, don't lie to me, you shitting on me because I'm a stripper. I'm good enough for you to fuck but not good enough for you to help get on. That's how it is, right?"

"I wasn't going to say stripper," he repeated.

"Then what the fuck was you going to say?"

"Hoodrat!" Javon barked back. "They ain't no fucking hoodrats. They don't come in my office smoking weed or talking shit. They're on time and they know how to conduct themselves in a professional manner."

"So now I'm a fucking hoodrat? Well, nigga, you come from the streets, too, don't forget that. Or is it that you already have?"

"I didn't come here to argue with you, Peaches."

"Then why did you come here, if I'm just some *fucking hoodrat*?"

"I'm starting to wonder the same shit."

"That's fucked up." Peaches closed her eyes. The silence in the room was suffocating the both of them. "Tell the truth Javon, are you fucking that girl?"

"You just don't get it. It's not her, Peaches, she's not the problem." Javon was frustrated. He hadn't come here to argue with Peaches but he had allowed himself to be dragged into it anyway.

"Oh, I get it, nigga. You think you too fucking good for me, now. That's why you been avoiding me. You done found you a little industry bitch, and now I can't get even get a call back."

"It would be better if I just leave."

She changed her tune real quick. "Where are you going? You ain't even going to stay with me while I'm in the hospital?"

"I got something to take care of," Javon replied, making his way to the door.

"That' s fucked up, Javon. You foul, muthafucka!" She continued to shout at him as the door shut behind him. Then she broke down in tears. "You ain't shit, nigga," she sobbed through the tears. "You ain't shit, and your ass will be back when the stuck up bitch see you ain't nothing but a hoodrat, *just like me, nigga!*"

THIRTY-SEVEN | The past week had been a busy

one for Fatima. She had made appearances at all the major record stores and a number of interviews on the early morning news shows. Craig had her scheduled for 106th & Park next week, and MTV the week after that.

Unofficially, Fatima's debut CD, "A Daughter's Song," was rumored to be close to platinum, and her first single, "Lonely When I'm With You," was tearing up the airwaves. It was on the top ten rotation at all the major market radio stations, and that was without the video. The video was due to drop next week on BET. Once the video hit, which by the way, was featuring super model Johnny Pierce as her love interest, the song was bound to crack the top ten video request list.

All in all, Fatima was excited. Even all the early morning wake ups and late night preps hardly put a damper on her energy. To her, she was living out a script she had long ago written and discarded hopelessly…proof that miracles do happen.

"Here we are." Craig came strutting into the office with the week's tally sheets rustling in his hands. From the smile on his face, it was bound to be good news. "Gather around, everyone, I want you all to hear this."

The room was mainly filled with office workers and a few of her label mates. She often wondered how the other artists on the label felt about the attention given to her. Most were older jazz musicians who had been in the music business for a few years, and had yet to see the popularity and fame that she and G-Rydah were bringing to the label. Not that they didn't have their own fan base. Jazz musicians, however, were like a small family. Everyone knew each other, knew the venues and even most of the really ardent fans.

Because her father was a jazz aficionado, Fatima had been introduced to the music at a young age. In making her album, she had combined jazz with African rhythms to create her own Sade type vibe. As a result, most of the jazz artists had taken a liking to her. The key to Fatima's success, however, was that like Alicia Keys and Jill Scott, she and the new crop of talented singers (and yes, talent had a lot to do with it) were able to add that Hip Hop flavor that propelled great music into a great modern art of expression. It not only touched the soul of the old, but it had the spirit of the youths captivated.

"According to the latest sound numbers, Fatima's debut CD, on Keynote Records, of course," Craig gave a little flourish of his arm and a slight bow, "has sold 835,000 copies in the first four days since its release and is estimated to go platinum by the weekend."

The room exploded into cheers. Everyone applauded the news. Fatima was swarmed with congratulatory hugs and handshakes. The pats on her back must have given rise to wings, because Fatima soon felt herself floating on cloud nine. All the hard work, disappointments and doubts she had lived with were misty colored memories fading into the background.

"Congratulations, Fatima." Craig gave her a hug. "I knew from the first time I heard you sing that you were meant for the big times."

"Every morning I thank God for the blessing, and I also thank you for believing in me," Fatima told him.

"Well, this is just the start. You know you are going to have to work even harder, now." Craig had reverted to his serious business tone. "Always remember, Fatima, fans are a fickle bunch of so and so. They can love you today and not even care to hear you tomorrow. You're only as good as your last hit."

"Well, then, we'll just have to keep on giving them nothing but hits," Fatima responded. Though she made light of the subject, she knew Craig was right. Anyone in the industry could point out plenty of short-lived success stories. The one hit wonders who rose to great heights seemingly overnight, then disappeared in a sea of mediocrity. Fatima had no intention of following that route. Too many people had sacrificed. Too many people had given up some part of themselves to see her succeed.

Fatima thought about her aunt, who had taken her in when she was a naïve and sometimes selfish little girl, and raised her as if she were her own daughter. Not that Fatima had been a problem child, but the culture shock of coming from a rural Tanzanian environment to the fast paced metropolises of the states had caused her a number of conflicts in itself. Her father's reputation just added to the scrutiny that she had to endure.

Then there was Solomon. Solomon, the one who had brought her back from the brink of hell and had restored her faith in herself. Would she even be here today if Solomon had not come into her life? But most of all she owed her Mama and Baba. From the day of her birth, both of them had put her needs before everything else. Baba had sent her to America so that she would have a chance to do something with her life. Having lost his wife, having to send his only child away must have torn his heart to shreds, but he did it for her. So that she might have a better life than he could provide for her.

No, Fatima had no intention of being a one hit wonder. She had too many people counting on her for her to fail. As she looked around the room, everyone was in a jovial mood, thinking about the success of the album, and of course, the money it would bring to the label. Fatima felt it in a different way. It wasn't about the money. To her, it was about fulfillment. She had been born to sing. Nothing else in the world brought her the joy she felt when she let her vocals flow, and now, she would be doing it for millions of people.

She closed her eyes and whispered, "Thank you, Mama."

THIRTY-EIGHT | The three of them sat at the table. Jah-Sun and T-Rock were having an animated conversation about a stripper named Paradise.

Derrick, however, was absorbed in his own thoughts. Things had been going good, in fact, they had been going better than good. In the South, E-Money was back in business, locking down North Carolina. The death of Johnny Junior put some heat on a number of operations, but E-Money, who had been laying low, was able to weather the storm. Now, he was back on the scene, building up the clientele and the funds were really flowing.

Over in B-More, Black was expanding a lot quicker than anyone had thought possible. The recent fall of one of Baltimore's major drug kingpins left a void for Black to step into without much drama.

Here in New York, Jah-Sun and T-Rock, two of Derrick's lieutenants, were stepping it up big time. They had been taking some of the young thugs in their crews up to Binghamton and Ithaca, New York to hustle. Derrick still kept an iron grip on the spots in Brownsville and East New York, but it was out of town work that was really paying off.

Last time he had traveled down to Florida to see his connect, he had brought them $750,000 in cash. $250,000 was owed; the other $500,000 was money to cop with. In the eight months' time Derrick had been dealing with this Miami connection, he had increased his purchases five times over. The connect took notice.

They were smart men. They understood the power of money and so they treated Derrick as the valued customer he was. He was often their VIP guest at many of the South Beach clubs and Miami hot spots.

In New York, it was a well-known secret that Derrick was amongst the ranks of the elite ballers. By most standards, he maintained an almost inconspicuous lifestyle. Many assumed he invested his money, or perhaps had it stashed away in some secret bank account in the Cayman Islands. Derrick shared personal info with few trusted comrades only. That's how he stayed two steps ahead of his competition. Derrick was respected by his enemies and loved by his associates, yet feared by both.

As Derrick sat there amongst his people, his thoughts were invariably on Javon. Though he still spoke with Javon regularly, in the last month he had only seen him once, by accident, at a South Beach Club, and once at Javon's house. When Javon had implied that he was getting into the music industry, it never registered with Derrick that it would affect their plans in the drug game, but it was. It had always been Derrick's dream to be the biggest dealer on the East Coast. He wanted to succeed where his father had failed. Over the years, he and Javon had worked their way up the ladder the hard way. Now, when everything they had been fighting for was in reach,

Javon was nowhere in sight.

Derrick, for the last two months, had been running the operation by himself. He knew Javon's absence wouldn't hurt things. They had put their operation together in such a way that even if neither of them were around, it would continue to flow, as long as the drugs were available. But, even as well as everything was going, Javon's absence took away from the excitement. This was their empire and Derrick couldn't understand Javon's desire for any other.

Derrick knew Javon's entry into the music world was paying

off. The gangsta rapper, G-Rydah, and the other artist he was involved with, all looked like they had the talent to be big stars. Derrick had seen them on a couple of TV specials and constantly heard their songs on all the radio stations. Still, he wondered how far Javon would make it in that game. He even wondered if he should have joined him when Javon asked, but history spoke against that. Javon wasn't the first hustler choosing to go that route and none before him had reached the same level of success they had in the drug game. If they did, it wasn't long before the Feds were sticking their nose in, looking for a way to bring them down.

Derrick had his doubts, but in the end, the cold, hard truth was Derrick loved the drug game too much to want to do anything else. Though he didn't have to, he still visited the spots occasionally and took pride in how efficiently they ran. He also took pride in how strong and loyal his team was. Derrick had been taught by old school hustlers that your workers had to be treated well, but punished severely when caught out of pocket, so he did both.

In total, he had close to 200 workers. All of them saw good money for their work. More importantly, Derek and Javon never stiffed any of their workers. If they saw a worker who was a real hustler and who knew how to get money, they would set him up in his own area or out of town, and let him do his thing. All they asked was that they cop their drugs from them. That was how Jah-Sun and T-Rock had climbed through the ranks. Though sometimes, Derrick did have serious doubts about T-Rock. T-Rock knew how to chase a dollar, but he was too flamboyant, in Derrick's opinion. Not to mention, he was a trick for pussy. Any nigga that thought with his dick was an eventual problem.

"Yo, Dee, what's up, homie? You zoning out on us?" T-Rock interrupted Derrick's train of thought.

"You know, got a lot on my mind. So what's the news with Gotti?"

"Them crackers ain't giving him no bail. You know how it is. He's Upstate pushing that shit in their town and he already got a record, so they know if he gets out on bail, it's a wrap. He ain't coming back."

"Police, bwoy, dem no like wen man a come from city to sell drug inna dem town."

Jah-Sun's accent was deep Jamaican. Derrick liked him because he was disciplined. Jah-Sun always carried himself in a militant manner.

"Uno fi git da bwoy a lawyer ta represent 'im," Jah-Sun commented.

"I'm working on that, Rasta man," T-Rock answered, irritated by the comment.

"What do you mean you're working on it? You got Gotti sitting in an Upstate county jail with a bullshit appointed lawyer?" Derrick couldn't believe T-Rock was playing one of his best soldiers like that.

"Homie, I got him. I'm going to take care of it. I just had to straighten out my money matters first. I lost a half a key when he got knocked," T-Rock said.

"Dem tings there should 'av set up in add-vance," Jah-Sun added, while rolling some weed.

T-Rock didn't respond, but he felt the fucking Yard man was trying to show him up in front of Derrick, and he didn't like that.

"Did you hit his people off with some paper for him?" Derrick asked.

"I was planning on going by his girl's house while I was down here," T-Rock explained.

"That I man believe," Jah-Sun said sarcastically.

Derrick turned to eye T-Rock before commenting.

"T-Rock we're a family, and family take care of their own. So I know I can count on you to do the right thing for Gotti, right?"

"Yeah, you know that, Dee; don't pay this Buju Bonton nigga

no mind. I'm going to take care of Gotti."

"One thing, T-Rock, just for conversation sake. I know that Gotti's girl is a dime piece. So with him not around, niggas are going to be pressing on her. The way I see it, it's her pussy so what ever happens is her decision. Know what I mean?" Derrick looked T-Rock in the eyes.

"Yeah, I feel you, Derrick," T-Rock answered tentatively.

"Nevertheless, family don't disrespect family like that. There's too many other women out here for a nigga to touch something that belongs to a homie. You know what I mean?" Derrick's message was clear.

"Yeah, Derrick. You know we don't get down like that," T-Rock stated.

"I know we don't, like I said, it was just conversation."

Derrick went back to sipping his drink, satisfied that T-Rock understood not to cross the lines that dictate so much in this game.

Triple Crown Publications presents . . .

THIRTY-NINE | "You okay?" The question stirred

Peaches from her thoughts. Turning toward Tamel, she smiled and let her hand rest on his thigh.

"I'm cool, baby, just had a long night. Thanks for the ride home."

"I told you before, Peaches, whatever you need, I'm there for you."

"I know, sweetie, and I appreciate it."

Though Tamel was trying to do the right thing by her, Peaches couldn't help it, her thoughts kept coming back to Javon. As far as she was concerned, he had really betrayed her. She had felt he was fucking that Fatima bitch ever since she saw them all hugged up in that *Source* magazine. But she wanted to give him the benefit of the doubt. Besides, she was a big girl. She knew niggas chased pussy, even when they had some at home. She could live with that. He never put no ring on her finger, so there wasn't much she could say. She was willing to let little indiscretions slide, as long as he took care of home base, and didn't flaunt shit in her face. But that wasn't good enough for the nigga. Nah, this nigga came back and shitted. He couldn't even wait until she got out of the hospital.

"These niggas ain't shit," Peaches mumbled to herself.

"What?" Tamel turned to look at her.

"Nothing, sweetie, I was just thinking out loud."

"Peaches, I know you got a lot on your mind, but like I said, you can count on me. I only wish I had been there when them niggas jacked you."

"Yeah, I wish you'da been there, too. I'd probably still have my car."

Tamel slowed down and pulled up in front of Peaches' apartment building. He double parked and turned to look at her. He was young, but the desire in his eyes was all man. Peaches loved when a man looked at her that way. It let her know he would do anything to please her.

Funny thing is, Javon used to look at her like that, too, and look how that turned out. She hadn't even heard from him since that afternoon in the hospital. Just thinking about him was starting to irritate her.

She started to open the door when Tamel reached over and took her hand.

"You sure you don't want any company?" he asked.

"Tamel, sweetie, I wouldn't be good company. I'm feeling kind of stressed."

"That's even more reason to let me come take care of you." He looked at Peaches, hopefully waiting for her to make a decision that would take them to another level.

Peaches knew that Tamel was sincere, but she also knew that most niggas were sincere when they wanted something. It's when they got it that the games would begin. She wasn't about to let herself get played again.

"Tamel, right now it's all about me. If you can deal with that, then you can come in. If you can't, then it's best you keep it moving." That would be his warning, Peaches told herself.

"I can deal with that," he said.

"I mean it, Tamel, I've been through a lot lately and I don't have no time for no bullshit," she said sternly.

"I can deal with it, Peaches." He grabbed her hand and squeezed it reassuringly.

"Okay then, let's go."

Peaches opened her car door, grabbed her bag, then stepped out onto the sidewalk. As she made her way to the house, she didn't bother looking back to see if he was following. She knew he was; she had heard the car door slam and the alarm beep. By the time he caught up she already had the key in the front door.

Peaches took a sideways glance his way as she opened the door. She couldn't front, he did look good, but he was young, probably no older than twenty by her estimation. Nowadays, though, little niggas were out on the streets and in the grind by the time they hit their teens. So, twenty came with a little more experience than you'd imagine. From the rocks on his rings and his chain, Peaches knew he was seeing some kind of paper, and if you were old enough to handle your business on the street, then it was all gravy far as she was concerned.

Peaches led Tamel into the apartment.

"Grab a seat on the sofa. The remote is on the end table."

Peaches walked into her bedroom, dropped her bag on the bed and dug into her dresser drawer. She had about a half an ounce left in a Ziploc sandwich bag. She grabbed two blunts off the dresser and went back into the living room. Tamel was sitting on the sofa flipping through the channels. He watched Peaches as she walked toward him, which Peaches found sort of cute.

"Here, roll up some weed. I got beer in the fridge. If you want some hard stuff, I got Bacardi in the kitchen cabinet over the sink." She dropped the bag of weed and two blunts on the coffee table. "I'm going to take a quick shower, so make yourself at home."

She turned and walked to the bathroom. She didn't have to look back to know he was watching. She had that kind of ass that every man watched when she was in motion. For Tamel's viewing pleasure, she threw a little more switch in her walk. She knew he was enjoying it.

Two minutes later, Peaches was completely naked and in the

shower. As the hot water massaged her body, she thought about Sandra. She would talk about her for days if she knew Peaches had Tamel in her house. She was such a slut when it came to these young ballers. Always talking about how she had this nigga or that nigga in training. Peaches laughed. As crazy as Sandra was, she didn't go through all the drama that Peaches was always going through, so she had to give her credit.

Peaches finished her shower, then lotioned her body in front of the full-length mirror which hung from the back of the bathroom door. She examined herself. Her stomach was still flat. Her hips were wide, but with her tiny waist, it gave her the most incredible curves. Her thighs were thick, but firm. She thought maybe a little too thick, but all the men in the club loved them. Her ass was perfect, and her tits still held up nice. Peaches knew she looked better than a lot of those video girls she saw on TV. The least Javon could have done was plug her in with one of the directors, but the muthafucka didn't even do that.

She looked at her face. It had healed up good, no scars. Well, just a tiny one on her right cheek, but it was barely noticeable. In the club, you couldn't see it at all. Anyway, it was a small price to pay. Who knows what would have happened if the girls hadn't come out when they did.

Peaches started to think that maybe having Tamel around wasn't too bad an idea. Those punks surely wouldn't have tried to jack her car if he had been around. Before she let Tamel get too comfortable with the idea of being around her, she was going to have to be sure that he knew who was in charge.

She wrapped a towel around her body and walked out of the bathroom. Tamel was sitting on the sofa smoking a blunt and sipping on a beer. It was training time. She walked over to him, stopping when she was standing between his legs.

"Can I smoke?" she asked him.

He looked up at her and passed her the blunt. She took two

tokes and let the herb ease her tension. With the blunt gripped in her right hand, she let her left hand fall down to the top of his head and started playing in his hair.

"Baby, do you want to stay with me tonight?" she asked him.

"Yeah, if that's what you want."

"But you have to know, if you stay, we do things my way, and that means you won't be fucking me tonight. Do you still want to stay?"

"Yeah, I'll stay."

Peaches smiled. He had passed her first test. She wanted to see if he'd leave when she told him he wasn't going to get his dick wet. But it was also the truth. Peaches had no intention of fucking him that night. Tonight, she was a selfish bitch, and she wasn't caring about no one else but herself.

"Good, 'cause I want you to stay." She bent down and kissed him on the top of his head. "In fact, I'm going to feed you."

"Feed me?"

"Yeah." Still standing between his legs, she took a deep toke on the blunt and blew the smoke toward the ceiling. She undid the towel and let it fall to the floor. Standing completely naked before him, she lifted her right leg to rest on the arm of the sofa and with her left hand, which was still in his hair, she pulled his face in between her legs. "Tonight, you get to eat Peaches." She winked flirtatiously at him.

Tamel hesitated for a second, then Peaches felt his tongue searching in her wet spot. She was pleased. He had passed her second test.

Triple Crown Publications presents . . .

FORTY | Craig had brought many of his artists down to Atlanta with him to participate in Fatima's video shoot. This was the video for her second single, "Ghetto Miseries," which she had done with G-Rydah. It was sure to become a street anthem. BET had sent a crew to cover the making of the video for an upcoming "All Access" episode. A couple of Keynote Jazz artists had also contributed to the track, and along with a few other industry celebrities, were making the trip for their cameos. Both Fatima and G-Rydah had quickly become big names in the industry, and other big-name celebrities from the worlds of sports, music and movies were often calling them to hang out. Fatima was amazed at how even walking down the street, she had begun to draw crowds of fans who recognized her and wanted her autograph.

Today was sure to be a hectic day. Her support system, Aaliyah and Brooklyn, had flown down to be with her. Fatima always kept them near, because they kept her grounded. They reminded her that friends are the ones who are there when fame and fortune are only dreams a million miles away from reality.

Craig and Javon were in their trailer, entertaining Chris Baylor. He was once a big star but had fizzled after his second CD dropped. He was from Atlanta and had stopped by, hoping to get in on the action. The three men were sharing some beers and opinions about the state of music, when Fatima knocked on the trailer door.

"Craig, can I come in?" Fatima asked.

"Sure, sweetheart, come on in. I got someone I want you to meet."

Fatima opened the door and climbed into the trailer. Her mind went into a state of shock when she saw who stood before her.

"Fatima this is ..." Craig started to make the introductions.

"Chris Baylor!" Fatima finished the sentence for him.

"Yeah," Craig stated, puzzled by Fatima's reaction. "You know each other?"

Fatima didn't answer the question. She felt none of this was real. She thought she was caught up in some time warp that had stripped away reality and transported her back to that place where she was just that worthless little black girl who no one believed in.

"Fatima ..." Chris reached out for her, and that movement snapped her from her trance.

She turned and ran. He had come back to destroy everything she had worked for. Fatima didn't know where she was running to, but she knew she had to get away. Chris ran after her, while Javon and Craig were immobilized by surprise.

"What just happened?" Javon asked, bewildered.

"I don't know, but you go after them, I'll call security," Craig responded.

"Fatima!" Chris shouted, as he caught up with her. Grabbing her roughly by the arm, he turned her around. "You still acting like a fucking kid!" he spat.

"Let go of me!" she screamed, as tears filled her eyes.

"Listen, you stupid bitch, I was the first one to give your black ass a chance, so now it's time for your ass to return the favor." He tightened his grip.

"Let her go!" Javon demanded. He didn't know what was going on, but from the way this guy was grabbing Fatima, he didn't like it.

"Ah, man, you got it wrong. Me and Fatima go way back, ain't that right, Fatima?"

Fatima said nothing but continued to shed tears.

"One more time, homie, let her go," Javon commanded, the anger in his voice clear.

"What you getting all bent out of shape for? Oh, I get it, you fucking her huh? Well, let me school you, homie. She was sucking my dick long before you even knew her. I'm the nigga that made her," Chris responded arrogantly.

Javon probably heard only half of his words before charging him. His swing connected on the side of Chris' head, sending him sprawling to the ground. Javon was over him immediately, ready to stomp him into the ground, when Craig showed up with security.

"Javon don't!" Craig shouted. "Let security handle it!"

Javon stepped back and watched as two burly men in black T-shirts that read "Security" picked Chris up and escorted him off the set. Javon turned to Fatima, who sat on the ground, crying.

"You all right?" he asked her.

Her head hung between her bent knees as her back heaved with her sobs. A crowd began gathering around.

"Craig, I'm going to take her to her trailer." Javon scooped Fatima up and made his way to her trailer. Once inside, he laid her down on the sofa and tried to calm her. Javon had never seen her behave like this before and was genuinely concerned.

"Fatima, what's going on with this guy?" Javon asked.

"Nothing. It doesn't matter, anyway."

"It does matter. Fatima, we care about you," he reassured her.

"Yeah, sure, everybody cares about Fatima," she replied sarcastically.

"What's wrong with you? Why you acting like that? I'm trying to help you," Javon retorted, frustration creeping into his voice.

"Help me? Javon who are you kidding? You're here to help yourself like everybody else. You're just like him."

"What?"

"You want to know the truth, Javon? Yeah, I sucked his dick, and I let you fuck me. Same difference, so I guess that's the price I had to pay to get where I'm at now."

"Fatima, I never said you had to fuck me to get anywhere."

"You didn't have to. Your actions spoke louder than your words."

"You crazy? When did I ever come at you like that?"

"Forget it."

"Nah, fuck that. When did I ever come at you like that?"

"What about the night in Hollywood, a couple of months ago. What was all that about?"

"What? You're the one that kissed me first."

"So now I'm the hoe?"

"I didn't say that." Javon was getting more frustrated with the way this conversation was going.

"So what are you saying?"

"Fatima, I have a lot of respect for you. I would never call you a ho. That night, I thought you wanted us to...I mean, for months we had been feeling each other out...I just thought it was what we both wanted."

"Then why did you leave? Why did you say it was no big deal?"

"Because of Solomon, that's why."

"Solomon?!"

"Yeah, you called his name in your sleep."

Fatima looked at Javon, then hung her head down and sobbed silently. Javon reached out to hold her and she moved into his arms.

"Javon, Solomon is dead."

"Dead?"

"Yeah, he died years before I even knew you."

"I didn't know," Javon mumbled.

"Solomon was Aaliyah and Brooklyn's brother. We were in love, but he was killed by drug dealers."

"Drug dealers killed him?"

"Yeah, he and some other guys were trying to clean up the community from the dealers. One night they came through and shot his best friend. He wanted to go even the score. I begged him not to go, but he wouldn't listen. He never came back alive. They found his body in a vacant building. That was years ago, Javon; he's part of my past. Why didn't you say something?"

"Stupid pride, I guess. I was hurt that it wasn't my name you were calling that night. I thought he was some other guy you were seeing."

"Damn, all this time I thought—"

"Shh, let's not worry about that anymore. We made some mistakes, but we can change things now for the better. Fatima, I love you and I want to be here for you. No more games. It's all about us, trust me. I need you to trust me."

Fatima looked up into Javon's face. For years she had wanted to be loved. To have her happy ending. She wanted to trust him. Looking into his eyes she saw their future and she knew she could believe in him.

They kissed and discovered a new destiny.

Triple Crown Publications presents . . .

FORTY-ONE | Peaches had her hands full with bags.

It seemed every time she and Tiffany spent time at the mall, they did it up. She really didn't mind. As long as Tiffany was happy, it was all good. Of course, Nana would complain, as usual, when they got home, but she'd deal with that later. Right now, the smile on Tiffany's face was all that mattered.

"Mommy, can I get my hair done at the beauty shop?"

"At the beauty shop?" Peaches looked quizzically at her daughter. "I thought Nana did your hair?"

"She does, but I thought it would be nice to get it done at the beauty shop. Besides, Nana might be tired of doing it." Tiffany looked up at her mother.

"Did she tell you she was tired?" Peaches asked, worried that Nana was having second thoughts about caring for Tiffany.

"No, mommy, it's just that my friend Chantel gets her hair done in the beauty shop, and they always make her look good, so I thought if you didn't mind, I could get my hair done there, too."

"Baby, you always look good," Peaches assured her.

"Aaww, Ma, you're supposed to say that. You're my mommy."

"Well, it's still true, but if you want to go to the beauty shop, I'll take you this week, okay?"

"Thank you, Mommy." Tiffany hugged Peaches as they walked through the mall.

Tiffany never knew her father. By the time Peaches was in the delivery room, she had realized that further hopes of JT coming back to take care of her were useless. If she and her daughter were going to make it in this world, it was going to be because she was going to make it happen. It was that day, amidst labor pains and screams of anguish, that the tiny cries of her daughter filled her with a firm resolve.

Later on that night, after the nurses had cleaned her baby up and brought her back to Peaches' waiting arms, Peaches made two promises. One was that her baby would never want for anything. The other was that no nigga would ever use her again without paying her price. She gave her heart, soul and body to JT and he had trampled over her and left her broken and soiled. It would not happen again.

Looking down at her newborn child, precious and fragile, Peaches thought about the Tiffany bracelet one of her boyfriends had given her. It had always been her most prized possession, until the day she pawned it to give JT money for his car. *How ironic*, she thought. She had given him the most precious thing she had. The only thing he had ever given her was the little girl she held in her arms. When the nurse asked Peaches if she had chosen a name for her baby she didn't hesitate. "Tiffany," she responded. Her most prized possession.

"Are you hungry, baby?" Peaches asked as they passed a Wendy's.

"A little, Mommy."

"Okay, let's stop and get something to eat."

Peaches loved spending time with her daughter. She spoiled Tiffany rotten and made sure that no part of her other life as a stripper tainted their special world together.

They walked into Wendy's, ordered and ate.

For the next half hour, they laughed and discussed mother and daughter things. Peaches knew she would soon have to school her daughter to the ways of men. They were dogs, and if you gave them too much leash, they would eventually misbehave. She would have to protect her baby from having to learn the hard way.

They finished their meal and continued their stroll through the mall. Tiffany continued excitedly looking at all the latest fashions and sharing girl talk with her mother. Peaches, however, was only half listening. Her thoughts had drifted to Javon. She had forgotten her golden rule and had allowed her heart to get caught up. And once again, another dog-ass nigga had fucked her around and kicked her to the curb. She had to laugh at herself for thinking that Javon had cared about her. He was as smooth as silk. She had to admit that, but in the end, just like every nigga she ever fucked with, he wasn't shit. To make matters worse, he had played her for some fake-ass Lauren Hill wannabe.

That's the part that Peaches really couldn't understand. What the fuck was Javon doing with that stuck up bitch? Javon never directly revealed his affair to Peaches, but she wasn't stupid. She knew he was in the streets doing his dirt to get his paper. That's why she fucked with him; he understood the grind, so she knew he wouldn't sweat her about how she got her paper. After all, he was in the hood getting his, too. But now, the nigga was trying to go Hollywood. Leaving her for some bitch who probably wouldn't survive a day on the streets. Javon was playing himself. She'd make him regret his choice.

"Mommy, Mommy." Tiffany was pulling Peaches by the hand into the record store. "Can I get this new CD?"

Peaches looked up to see a giant poster of a chocolate-brown, dread-locked sista that read "Fatima: Afrikan Empress of Soul" and underneath, the words "A Daughter's Song." She stared at the poster, thinking that Javon would definitely regret his choice, more sooner than later.

Triple Crown Publications presents . . .

FORTY-TWO | "Girl, pass the blunt," Peaches said, reaching over the coffee table.

"Damn, you act like I'm going somewhere," Sandra answered.

"Nah, bitch, you act like you forgot I'm smoking, too."

"Well, all you had to do is roll up another one, with your thirsty ass. Shit, this one was getting me right," Sandra said, passing the blunt to Peaches.

"I know you right. Where you get this weed from?" Peaches asked.

She and Sandra were relaxing at Sandra's place. Lil' Man was with his father and they had planned to just sit back and watch some DVDs.

"One of them young boys hustling on the corner. I got him in training right now." Sandra said with a slight laugh.

"Sandra! You really are scandalous. Them boys ain't nothing but babies."

"Girl, first of all, the boy is over eighteen, so don't even try that R. Kelly bullshit. And second, he's the one trying to holler at me, with his cute, young ass."

"So, you fucking him?"

"No. He's just in training. I told him to be a good boy and take care of mama, and when he turns twenty-one next year I'll fuck his brains out."

"Girl, you need to stop. That boy is too young for you."

"That's how I like them. Young, dumb and full of cum."

Sandra laughed out loud at her own remark.

Peaches, changing the subject, took the opportunity to bring up what was on her mind.

"Sandra, you want to go out to Jersey for a couple of nights? Jackie and Tia went to dance at a couple of clubs out that way and they said the money was really good. I'm getting tired of these same broke-ass niggas here."

"I don't care, long as it's someplace with class. I ain't dancing in no nasty-ass, back-room club."

"We can find us some good clubs. Ask your friend Big Mike if he'll go with us."

"You know I am. After what happened with you, I ain't taking no chances. Besides, after I get all worked up in them clubs, it's good to have a nigga around to spread this pussy."

"Damn, girl, is fucking the only thing you ever think about?" Peaches asked, taking another toke before passing back the blunt.

"The money, baby. I keep my mind on the money, too." Sandra took a toke. "You're just upset 'cause you ain't had no dick since pretty boy bounced." She blew the smoke toward Peaches.

"And how would you know who been in this coochie?" Peaches asked her sarcastically.

"Because you act like that shit is made of gold. You know how many times I tried to hook you up with some bona-fide ballers and you acted stuck up?"

"Stuck up?"

"Yeah, bitch, stuck up. Don't front like pretty boy didn't have that pussy on lockdown. You wasn't trying to fuck with no one else."

"That's not stuck up. Javon was my man."

"So what! These niggas will have a girl and still be out there fucking someone else on the side. Or have you forgotten already?"

"I ain't forgot shit. Besides, I don't want to talk about Javon. You fucking up my high with that bullshit."

"You see, that's what I'm talking about. I don't need no man if I'm going to be acting like that afterward. Satisfy your needs, sista girl, and let them go about their business. Anyway, if you want me to hook you up, let me know. Mike got some friends."

"I'm all right," Peaches answered, trying to let the subject go.

For the last month, she had been letting Tamel satisfy her needs, but she didn't want to tell Sandra that. Sandra was her girl, but to her, everything was topic for open discussion and Peaches didn't need or want her business all out on the streets. Besides, Peaches wasn't sure how far this thing with Tamel would go. For right now, he was taking care of her both financially and sexually, but she hadn't decided if she wanted that to become a permanent arrangement, yet. For right now, she just wanted to play everything by ear and see how things turned out. As long as she was the one calling the shots everything was gravy.

Triple Crown Publications presents . . .

FORTY-THREE | Derrick rolled up in East New

York to see Veronica. She'd called earlier on the cell phone, asking
him to pick her up. Unlike Javon, Derrick didn't keep a steady girl.
He didn't have time for it. The hustle was his girl, but Ronnie,
that's what everybody called Veronica, was his favorite shorty. She
was about that money, and she understood the game.

Derrick had met her out in Atlantic City a few years ago. She
was out there hitting pockets. Home-girl was a pro. If you
blinked, your wallet was gone. She also had looks that made the
big bank ballers take notice. She was thick in the hips and had ass
for days. When she walked, her movements were hypnotic. She
had little breasts, but Derrick wasn't a breast man, anyway.

Her one flaw was the scar on the side of her face. She had gotten cut in a scrape with some butch awhile back when she was in
Bedford Hills doing a bid for robbery. The scar wasn't big, but it
was noticeable. She still looked good, even with the scar. It made
her seem more street.

The most important factor that Derrick liked about her was
that she wasn't always in his business. When Derrick was with
Ronnie, they did them, and when he wasn't around, she did her.
She didn't sit around trying to find a way to lock a nigga down.
She knew Derrick was about his money, and she was about hers,
so they had a mutual respect for each other's space.

Tonight, she was supposed to meet Derrick at his apartment
in Crown Heights, but her car was acting up, so she asked him to

come get her. Javon had them on the guest list for the Brethren, (that was Keynote's male group) CD release party. Derrick wasn't into the party scene like that, but he hadn't seen Ronnie in a couple of weeks so this was the perfect opportunity to take her out and also see Javon. They had been slipping into their own worlds and hardly spent any time together anymore.

Veronica stepped out her front door wearing a three quarter length black mink coat, some black Ferragamo jeans, a beige Versace blouse and beige suede Manolo Blahniks. She had on an iced out tennis bracelet and platinum linked diamond earrings. Ronnie was definitely dressed to impress. The only difference between her and most of the rich, spoiled broads that would show up tonight was Ronnie's shit was the result of her fine tuned skills as a booster.

"You really put it on tonight," Derrick complimented her.

"You know I had to represent for you. Muthafuckas better recognize two of BK's finest," she replied.

"For sure."

Derrick started to walk to the ride, when out of the corner of his eye, he saw the move. Just as he turned to look, the sawed off barrel of a shotgun was leveling his way. Derrick turned to face the shooter pulling his gun and throwing his body to the right. Derrick crashed into Ronnie taking them both to the ground as the shotgun blast tore over them. He felt the breeze and knew that the next one wouldn't miss. The shooter was about fifteen feet away. Derrick let off three rapid shots hitting him in the chest.

Just as Derrick got up, he heard the next shot, but he was too late to turn. It tore through his left shoulder, knocking him into the bushes. The gun slipped from his grip tumbling out of sight. There had been another shooter somewhere in front of him, but in his haste to deal with the one who had been on his peripheral, he hadn't seen the one directly in front of him. The mistake could prove to be a fatal one if he didn't do something quick.

The pain was tearing through his shoulder, but he had to get up and find his gun. Painfully, Derrick managed to climb out of the bushes. He saw his gun laying in the walkway. The shooter saw it, too. He was older than Derrick, and looked Spanish.

This obviously wasn't a stick up. Stick up kids don't shoot first, they shoot as a last resort. Which meant that this was a hit. These cats were gunning for Derrick, and he wasn't even sure if there were more of them waiting for him to stand up again and show himself.

Derrick couldn't get back to the building, so his only option was to try and reach his gun. Derrick crawled to the end of the bushes. He was only going to get one chance, so he couldn't fuck it up. He perched himself at the end of the walkway, still hidden by the bushes. He concentrated on the shooter's footsteps, took a deep breath and got ready to lunge for the gun. Just as he leapt from the bushes, he heard the gunshots. One, two, three, four shots rang out. It was a small caliber gun, but Derrick realized they couldn't be shooting at him or he would have been hit by now.

He reached his gun, and with it in hand, turned to see Ronnie firing at the would-be hit man, the shooter saw her, too, and turned his gun on her. He got off one shot before Derrick's shot hit him in the side of the head. Derrick got up more carefully this time, looking for more shooters. Ronnie lay in the grass. The gunman's last shot had grazed her. Derrick made his way to her.

"You okay?" he asked.

"I think so. Damn, my coat is fucked up."

"Don't worry about that now. Let's get out of here before the cops come."

They walked quickly to Derrick's ride. People were already peeping out the windows, but this was East New York, so gunshots were more or less an everyday event. It would be a while before the cops made their appearance.

"You drive." He passed Ronnie the keys.

"Where we going? Brookdale or Kings County?"

"Neither. I can't walk up in no hospital with gunshot wounds. There's two bodies laying out here. Police ain't that stupid. "

"We got to do something, Dee. You're bleeding, and ain't no telling how much damage that bullet did."

Ronnie was right, but Derrick knew going to a hospital was out of the question. He couldn't go to his apartment, either, until he knew what this was about. They might have someone waiting there.

"Okay, drive out to Queens," he instructed her.

"Where to?"

Derrick didn't want to tell her the address to the safe house, but he was losing blood, and no telling how bad he was hit.

"Drive out to Inwood and 106th."

Derrick reached for his cell phone and speed dialed Javon's number. He heard it ringing but everything else was fading. All around him, the dark edges were closing in and swallowing him up. The last word he heard was Javon's hello, then everything went dark.

FORTY-FOUR | Peaches sat on her living room sofa

watching the 54-inch, high definition television Tamel had purchased for her. She smiled, thinking to herself that the little nigga was definitely on his job. Since Peaches had started fucking Tamel he had been paying out like a slot machine. He no longer came to the club, because he did not want to see her dancing with other men. Of course, that was his problem.

The first time he brought the subject up, Peaches had looked him straight in the eyes and told him in no uncertain terms, that if he ever again tried to tell her what to do, she would kick his ass to the curb. That was good enough to keep him in line. With no other choice, he decided to stay out of the club. At first, Peaches thought she had played herself. She worried about the money. After all, he was the best of her customers, but in the end, it all worked out for the best. When she called him he came over to the house, and when she asked him for money, he gave her what she asked for. In return, Peaches fucked him. Not just sexed him, she really turned his young ass out in ways she knew would keep him coming back. Thinking about it now caused Peaches to laugh.

So what if I'm a freak; I'm a well-paid freak, she thought to herself, as she continued to laugh about it.

Peaches took a sip of her beer, still slightly amused with herself, then reached for the remote control and flipped to BET. Leaning back on the sofa to watch 106th & Park, she continued to think about Tamel. Thoughts of him always made her horny. It wasn't the sex that did it. It was the power she felt. She loved the control she had over him. She understood part of it was her age. She was seven years older than Tamel, and psychologically he tended to give in to her demands, almost as if she were his mother. She liked that. Sometimes, she saw herself as the teacher, showing him how to please and be pleased. Other times, she felt kinky, almost depraved. As if Tamel were an innocent child that she was corrupting. The truth was somewhere in the middle.

Though Tamel was a disciple of the streets, he was immature when it came down to women. Give him a gun, drugs or any of the other street paraphernalia, and he was comfortable with it. But left alone with her, Peaches could sense his nervousness, much in the same way a predator smells the fear of its prey. Still, it was that shy nervousness in her presence that excited her sexually. The knowledge that he was hers to mold, to control, her own private plaything. So she took advantage of it, and play with him she did.

Peaches started to reach for her phone, intent on calling her plaything over, when she heard the one name that above all else, she loathed.

"Let's welcome R&B's newest star, Fatima Amir, to 106 & Park."

The slim, half-dreadlocked, half-braided host was introducing that black-ass tramp who had stolen Peaches' man.

She couldn't believe it. Everywhere she turned, that no good bitch was there. Infuriated, she stared at the screen with malice. It wasn't just the fact that Javon had left her for this bitch. What really angered her was the bitch acted like her shit didn't stink. She probably thought everybody was supposed to fall over and kiss her black ass. Bet no one suspected that the bitch would take the next girl's man if she got a chance. Peaches didn't have any moral ethics to prevent her from doing whatever she desired. But at least she was woman enough to admit it. She didn't run around playing high and mighty.

Yet, no matter how much she hated the bitch, Peaches knew it was really Javon who had betrayed her. Fucking a stripper was all right when he was just another street nigga, but now that he was a big time music producer, he had tossed her aside for some so-called star's pussy. Well, like Sandra always said, a nigga will only do to you what you allow him to do to you.

Peaches decided it was time to teach Javon a lesson. He was about to learn the difference between an "industry" bitch and an "in-the-streets" bitch. She grabbed her phone and hit Tamel's number.

Triple Crown Publications presents . . .

FORTY-FIVE | "Hello … hello … I can't hear you …"

Javon was about to hang up when a rushed voice finally answered.

"Hello, who is this?" a female asked. The voice was not familiar to him.

"This is Javon. Who is this?"

"Jay, it's Ronnie. I'm with Dee. He got shot."

"What?!" Her words snapped Javon to attention.

"Where's Dee, Ronnie? And what happened?"

"He's right here in the car with me, but he's unconscious and losing a lot of blood."

"What hospital you going to? I'll meet you there."

"He said not to take him to a hospital. It's a big mess, Jay. Two other guys got laid down, and the cops will probably be all over the place any minute."

"Damn. So where you at now?"

"On my way to Queens. Dee said something about Inwood and 106th, but he didn't give me an address."

"Okay, don't worry about it, I know the place. Just park right on the corner when you get there. I'm going to phone ahead and have some people waiting for you when you reach there. I'll be over there myself as soon as possible."

Javon hung up the phone. Fatima was standing beside him. She had heard the conversation. No telling what she could piece together from just this end, but from the look on her face, she knew something was wrong.

"Fatima, I'm going to have to take care of some business. You should catch a cab and go to the party. I'll catch up with you later on tonight."

"Javon, what's wrong?"

"Nothing major, I just have to go see some people."

"Javon, I'm not stupid, I can see something is wrong."

"It's nothing. Excuse me a minute. I got some calls to make, then I'll call you a cab."

"Make your calls. When you're finished, then we'll talk." She walked away.

Javon called the safe house in Queens. Tommy Guns answered the phone. Javon explained to him what was going on and what to expect. When he walked back into the living room, Fatima was sitting on the sofa, head bowed in her hands.

"Fatima, let me take care of this and I'll see you later on tonight, okay?"

When she looked up, she had tears in her eyes. Javon kneeled down in front of her.

"Baby, what's wrong?" Her tear-stained face held Javon in a trance.

"I don't want to lose you," she whispered.

"Sweetheart, you're not going to lose me. I'll be back tonight." Javon wiped the tears from her eyes and kissed her wet face.

"Take me with you."

"I can't, Fatima."

"You said we had a commitment," she reminded him.

"We do, baby, but this ain't about us right now."

"Everything is about us." She grabbed Javon's hands. "Javon, you told me to trust you, and I do. Now I'm telling you to trust me."

"I do trust you."

"Then take me with you," she demanded.

It seemed to Javon that no matter how much he tried to keep

these two worlds apart they kept crashing into each other.

"Listen. There are certain things I'm trying to take care of in my life, and they're not things you should be involved in. So please, let me straighten out my business, then we can start off with a clean slate."

"Javon, there is no such thing as a clean slate. Whatever we've done, we've done. All we can do is live with the consequences of our actions, but though we can't erase our past, we can learn to make better choices in the future. I know that right now you are trying to protect me, but I don't need your protection. I need your love and I need your trust. Whatever it is you're going through, let's face it together. I got your back. I'm not going to abandon you."

It wasn't a good idea to take her. It wasn't because of the safe house—that was already blown when Derrick let Ronnie know what block it was on. It was really about Fatima, and what she represented. She was the clean get-away, the escape from the madness of this grind Javon was caught up in. Bringing her along would soil her. It would dirty any possibility of making a clean break from all this. But to not bring her meant the commitment was on shaky ground.

In the end, Javon did bring her along. After all, commitment is about loyalty, and Javon was a man who lived by principles.

Triple Crown Publications presents . . .

FORTY-SIX | "What the fuck you mean you're going to talk to him?" Peaches shouted. "That nigga violated us, Tamel! There is nothing to talk about!"

"Peaches…" Tamel tried to calm her down.

"Peaches, what?! That nigga grabbed my ass! I told him I was fucking with you and he laughed and grabbed my ass. He even told me straight to my face that he was going to come get some of this pussy so I wouldn't miss getting fucked by a real man. What kind of shit is that to say? He's violating you and he's violating me. Now are you going to stand there and let him play you like a little nigga, or are you going to man up?" she asked.

"I already told you, I'm going to handle it," Tamel retorted, irritated by her berating him.

"Nah, nigga, what you said was you was going to talk to him. Fuck talking to him! I want you to handle your business. If I'm giving this pussy to a nigga that can't hold it down, then let me know, 'cause there's enough real niggas trying to get in these panties!"

The disgust in her voice and look on her face stung him. Tamel jumped up from the sofa, body tense, adrenaline fueled by rage.

"Fuck you talking about Peaches? I know you ain't saying I'm scared of that nigga!" Peaches knew how far to push him. The first thing any woman learns is how far to push her man to get him to respond like she wants. This was an art Peaches had mastered long ago. She cautiously walked over to Tamel, wrapped her arms around his waist and leaned her body against his. With her head resting on his chest, she spoke soothingly to him.

"You my nigga, Tamel. I know you ain't scared of no one. But these niggas out here keep trying to whisper in my ear behind your back. Calling you a young nigga and trying to shoot down your status." She turned her head up and looked him in the eyes. "I don't know what kind of bitches you used to fucking with, but you got a thorough-ass bitch with you now, so you got to be a thorough nigga. Put that work in, baby. Make that nigga Javon the example. I can tell you how to get that nigga and get paid at the same time. Is you with that or what?"

Tamel looked into her eyes and understood the responsibility of having a girl like Peaches. She was real, and only a real nigga could hold her down. She needed him to represent for them. To let the streets know they weren't dealing with lames. He wouldn't let her down.

"I'm down, baby girl; fuck that nigga. I got something for his ass."

Peaches smiled and laid her head back on his chest.

FORTY-SEVEN | Javon reached the Inwood block of

South Jamaica Queens. Driving past the green and white three story private home he and Derrick routinely used as their safe house, he saw part of his crew camped out on the front porch. He continued around the block, circling it one time, attentive to his rearview mirror, just in case he was being followed. Certain he was safe, he pulled up on the corner and parked. Fatima was sitting on the passenger side, and hadn't said much during the ride. Javon was having second thoughts about bringing her along, but it was too late to do anything about it, now.

"You want to wait for me here?"

"No," she firmly announced. "I want to go with you."

Not wanting to argue, Javon opened the driver side door and stepped out of the car. He looked across the roof to see Fatima already getting out on her side. She hurried around the car and came to stand by him. Part of him was pleased that she was the kind of girl that would stick by her man when there was trouble. But he also realized that in this kind of lifestyle, standing by him wasn't exactly a safe place to be. Javon wished he had more time to reason with her, but right now he was more concerned with Derrick.

They made their way to the green and white house halfway down the block. Reaching the porch, he found Tommy sitting in a chair with his coat in his lap. From his vantage point he could see the coat was concealing a sawed off shotgun. Standing just inside the doorway was Junior, holding a Mac-11 machine gun.

"What's up? Where's Dee?" Javon asked as he walked through the gate.

"He's inside. Peanut's taking care of him," answered Tommy, taking a second glance, upon noticing who Fatima was. Javon walked into the house, followed by Fatima, leaving Tommy and Junior outside in a conspiratorial whisper, brought on by Fatima's presence. When Javon stepped into the living room, he found Veronica sitting by the window, smoking a cigarette. By the looks of her, she was upset, but working hard to keep control of her emotions. Peanut was in conversation with another woman, who Javon didn't know. Peanut was an old timer who lived in the neighborhood. He ran a game room down the block and kept an eye on the safe house for Derrick and Javon. He took care of things and kept his mouth shut, which is what they liked about him the most.

Javon walked over to Peanut, gave him a questioning look about the woman, and asked, "What's up?"

"She's all right ... this is Delores," Peanut introduced the woman. "She lives over on South Road. She's a nurse at Jamaica Hospital. I called her when I saw how bad Dee was bleeding."

"Where's he at?"

"We laid him down on the bed," Peanut replied.

"I did what I could to clean his wound up, but I ain't sure how bad the damage is until I can examine him in a hospital," Delores volunteered.

"Well, let me see him first," Javon said. Then, turning to Veronica, he asked, "Ronnie, are you all right?"

"Still alive," she answered. "What's going on, Jay? Who y'all at war with?"

"I couldn't tell you, Ronnie, but I'm definitely going to find out. Let me talk with Dee, and then I'll be back to take care of you."

Javon was upset with himself. He didn't know what was going on, or who the beef was with. Derrick hadn't mentioned anything the last time they had spoken, but still Javon felt if he had been around, he'd be more of a help.

He turned to face Fatima.

"Let me talk to my man for a minute, privately, okay?"

He could see she didn't want to leave his side, but she nodded reluctantly. Entering into the bedroom, he found Derrick lying on the bed with his eyes closed. Derrick was bare-chested and from his shoulder down the front side of his left chest, he was bandaged. His blood had soaked and spotted the white strips of cloth.

Derrick, sensing someone had entered the room, tightened the grip he had on the gun in his right hand and his eyes fluttered open.

"It's me, dawg," Javon assured him.

Derrick smiled at the familiar voice and relaxed his gun hand.

"The girl gave me some pain killers and they got me a little drowsy ... hard to keep my eyes open," Derrick explained.

"What's the deal? Who was it?" Javon asked.

"Don't know, didn't recognize any of them, but it was a hit."

"You don't think it could have been a stick up?"

"Nah, they came shooting first. They were laying for me or maybe following me...not really sure."

"How many?"

"Two Spanish cats, that I know of." Derrick was grimacing from the pain.

"Homegirl says you got to go to the hospital."

"Not a good idea. I left two bodies in front of Ronnie's building ... where is Ronnie?"

"She in the other room."

"Yo, Jay, she put that work in for real ... take care of her, that's my girl ... you should have seen her." Derrick smiled.

"Don't worry, I got her, but we got to do something about you first."

"Just stay on point, homie. Someone out there is coming at us and we can't be slipping." His eyes were nearly closed.

"Rest yourself, I'll take care of everything."

Javon walked out of the bedroom, trying to figure out his next move. In the living room, he found Fatima and Ronnie talking on one side of the room. On the other side Delores, Peanut and Junior were engrossed in a conversation of their own. All of it seemed to stop when Javon entered the room. It was clear that they were waiting for Javon to set things in motion. Javon walked purposely over to where Peanut stood.

"Let me talk to you," he said, pulling Peanut to the side. When they were a distance from everyone else, he laid the plan down. "I'm going to call Black Jack and tell him to bring the van around. You, Tommy and Black Jack clear the house out. All the guns, drugs, whatever you got in cash and the books, give it all to Black Jack, and give me a call when it's all done. I'm going to take Junior with me and cross over into Jersey with Derrick. Hopefully, we can get him into a hospital over there without too many questions."

"Okay, I'm on it. I'll start packing everything up now," Peanut assured him.

Javon made his way over to Fatima and Ronnie. He knew Ronnie had been through the ordeal with Derrick. The fact that she was still standing was probably more a testament to the hit man's focus on Derrick than anything else. Yet, he didn't want to send her back home until he knew for sure everything was cool.

"Ronnie, thanks for taking care of Derrick."

"Jay, you know that's my heart. He's going to be okay, right?"

"Yeah, it looks like it ain't too serious, but I'm going to take him to a hospital to make sure."

"Out here in Queens?"

"Nah, I'm going to try to slide into Jersey with him. Ronnie, you shouldn't go back to your place just yet."

"You think they're still out there?"

"Who knows, but if they're not, the police are bound to be all around snooping for witnesses. Better to lay low for now. You got someplace to stay for a couple of days?"

"I can stay with my girl. You're going to call me and let me know what the deal is, right?"

"Yeah, soon as I can straighten some things out and get Derrick taken care of, I will get at you. Here, take this." Javon reached in his pocket and pulled out a wad of money for her. "That should hold you for a couple of days. I'll check with you tomorrow, okay?"

"Thanks."

She gave Javon a hug, then pulled her cell phone out to call her girlfriend.

Javon turned to Fatima who had silently been playing the background. Though realization had come to everyone there that she was, indeed, Fatima Amir, platinum singer, the seriousness of what was going on had overshadowed her celebrity status, and precluded her from the normal attention her presence command-ed. Nonetheless, Fatima was satisfied playing the background, she knew this was Javon's moment of tribulation and she was there to support him.

"Fatima, I have to take my man to the hospital," Javon explained to her.

"Okay, I'll go with you."

"That's not a good idea. To be honest, I shouldn't have brought you along in the first place. You don't need to be involved in this mess; you got more to lose than anyone else. Besides, the less you know the better, in case the cops come around asking questions."

"Javon, you don't have to worry about me talking to the police. Besides, I don't know anything other than your friend needs help."

"Yeah, but what we don't need is attention. Fatima, we can't walk into a hospital with you there. Too many people would recognize you."

"Well, I was going to tell you that I had a better idea."

"Like what?"

"I know someone who could help."

"That'll just be involving more people."

"Trust me, Javon."

With those words she pulled out her cell phone and began dialing.

FORTY-EIGHT | Tamel sat in the car watching the

front door of the third house on the block. It was Javon's house–Peaches had described it perfectly. It was a nice, private home tucked in a quiet neighborhood behind Kings Highway. Still, with the money Javon was supposed to be holding, Tamel expected something bigger. Peaches had given Tamel the lowdown on that nigga, Javon. He was the baller, Derrick's partner, and the two of them were holding major paper.

Tamel put his homie, Killa, on to the move. Killa had his own score to settle with Derrick and saw this as his opportunity. Tamel had his doubts about fucking with Derrick, since he was a known gun man. He had shot Killa for nothing. He felt sure they could rob Javon with no problem, but he knew if Derrick was there, they'd have to kill him. Of course, that's exactly what Killa wanted to do, so shit was going to be on and popping if they both showed up.

"Yo, son, you sure these niggas are in town?" Killa asked. Tamel turned to look at Killa, who was in the backseat playing with a Game Boy.

"Yeah, Peaches called him this afternoon and told him she had to pick up some things she had left over there. She told him she was coming early tomorrow morning and he told her he'd be there. That means sometime tonight he has to come home, if he's going to be here to let her in tomorrow."

"It's already three in the morning. Son might have said fuck her, she can get her stuff some other time."

"Nah, I doubt it. Besides, the longer he takes, the better. Less people to worry about being up to witness anything. Also, the more likely he'll be tired or drunk and we can take him easily."

"I sure hope his bitch-ass partner is with him. I want to see how tough he act when he's on the other side of the gun," Killa commented.

"Just remember, we need to get inside that safe first, so don't start shooting until we get that combination."

Tamel was having second thoughts about bringing Killa along. Peaches told him there was at least half a million in that safe, and the last thing Tamel wanted was to miss out on that kind of easy money because Killa wanted to get back at that nigga, Derrick.

"Believe me, fam, I ain't trying to leave that paper behind." Killa responded.

What Tamel didn't know was that Killa had no intention of sharing that money, either. If things went according to his plan there would be three bodies in that house come morning: Derrick, Javon and Tamel.

"Do you think that shiesty bitch is telling the truth about that money?" Killa asked.

"Why would she lie?" Tamel reasoned.

"Who knows? You can't trust no bitch like that," Killa said offhandedly.

"Son, that's my shorty," Tamel said defensively.

Killa laughed. "The pussy that good? Well, nigga, you better sleep with both eyes open, 'cause if she set this nigga up, she'll do the same to you."

"Nah, son, it ain't like that with me and her."

"Whatever you say, homie." Killa shook his head in disgust and went back to playing the Game Boy.

FORTY-NINE | Fatima and Javon had to stay in the upstairs living room, while Fatima's people worked on Derrick's injuries in their basement facilities. As it turned out, Derrick's wounds weren't as serious as they looked. He had lost a lot of blood, so the doctor warned them against moving him around. They offered to let Derrick stay overnight to rest up. Javon wasn't sure that was a good idea at first but Fatima assured him that Derrick would be well taken care of. Besides, no one knew about the basement clinic, so he'd be safe there in case the police were looking for him.

The crazy realization hit Javon at that moment that Craig had been right. Fatima *was* connected to some kind of radical militia. How the hell else would she have access to some basement clinic nobody else knew about, and a doctor that didn't ask questions? Tonight, he had too much on his mind to think about it, but he stored the information in the back of his head for future reference. Leaving Derrick behind, they climbed into Javon's Benz.

"Listen, it's late, but I can still drop you off at the party or at your house if you like," Javon informed Fatima.

"Where are you going?"

"Home. I got to get some things together."

"Then I want to go with you."

"That's not a good idea."

"Why not?"

"Fatima, that's my boy laying up in there. Someone just tried to take him out, and it's not going to end like that. A lot of shit is about to hit the fan and you don't need to be around me right now."

"Javon, you need to think about what you're going to do. This ain't your lifestyle. You're a music executive, not some street thug."

"No, no, no! That's the problem, Fatima! This *is* my life and I've been running from it! Ducking, like I could get away from it, but every time I turn the corner, there it is smacking me in my face! My boy is laying in there shot up, and I don't even know what is going on! Do you know why? Because I'm too busy running around fronting, like I'm Puff Daddy or somebody!" Javon paused to calm himself. "I tried, Fatima, believe me, I tried, but like you told me earlier, our past can't be erased."

"No, it can't be erased, but we can make better decisions. Javon, I love you, and I don't want to lose you."

"I love you, too, but what's love without loyalty? What kind of man would it make me if my homie's blood was spilled and I didn't do anything about it? Understand me, sweetheart, I have to take care of this. After that, we can talk about our future."

Fatima felt it happening again. Deja vu of Solomon walking away to his death. This time, she was determined not to let it go down that way again. She knew if she could stay with Javon tonight, she could calm him down and convince him to find another way in the morning. If she let him go, there's no telling what would happen. He had made his choice, now, she had to make one. This was her fork in the road and she wasn't going to make the same decision that lost her Solomon.

"Okay, Javon, I respect your decision. But I'm still going with you tonight," she said adamantly.

"Fatima, this is not a game."

"I understand that, but if you're just going home, then let me stay with you tonight, and tomorrow, you're free to take care of your business."

Javon considered it and saw no harm in it. It was too late to go out looking for who ever was responsible, and besides, by tomorrow, Derrick would be in better shape and could help figure out who was coming at them.

"Okay. For tonight only."

As he revved the engine up and began the journey home, he laid his nine millimeter in his lap and covered it with his jacket. It was always better to be prepared, just in case.

Triple Crown Publications presents . . .

FIFTY | "Yo! Here they come!" Tamel spotted the white Benz as it turned the corner.

Killa dropped the Game Boy and grabbed the Tech nine he had laid on the backseat next to him. He looked at the car slowing down in front of the house. He could make out two people.

"That's what's up! That punk-ass nigga, Derrick, is with him! Yo, Ta, you take the driver and I got the passenger side!" Killa exclaimed, excited at the idea of finally showing the nigga who shot him how real niggas come back.

"Remember, let's get them inside the house as quick as possible, and then we can take care of business," Tamel reminded him.

"Nigga, who the fuck you think you talking to? I know what the fuck I'm doing. Just make sure you don't slip up."

Killa was fed up with Tamel's scary ass. If he thought he could handle Derrick and Javon by himself, he'd shoot this stupid nigga now, and step to this shit alone. But he knew it would be difficult to get the drop on both of them, especially if they were both strapped. As soon as the car parked, Tamel and Killa were out of their ride and stepping to Javon's Benz.

Javon turned the car off. His mind was on what Fatima had said earlier. She was right, in a way, about making decisions. Whoever shot Derrick had to pay, but he had to move smart. He had too much on the line, including Fatima, to toss it all away thinking emotionally. He gripped the gun in his lap, feeling it's weight, wondering why it always had to come to this. Then, he turned to look at Fatima. When their eyes locked, he knew there wasn't any real choice. The gun would only bring more pain and suffering, but Fatima, that was his real future. He had to resolve this in a way where he didn't lose her.

Before he could continue that thought, his door was jerked open. He turned in time to see a light-skinned kid pointing a gun at him with one hand and reaching to snatch him out with the other. Javon didn't have to reach for his gun; it was already in his hand. The kid didn't even notice it, until Javon pulled the trigger. The gunshot echoed loudly in the quiet of the early morning. The slug found its target with an impact strong enough to send the kid crashing backwards to the sidewalk. Javon watched it all in slow motion, like a movie. Then, all hell broke loose.

As Killa opened the passenger door he shoved the Tech nine into Derrick's neck, except, when he looked, it wasn't Derrick. For a second, Killa was confused, he was expecting Derrick but it was some bitch. He felt a pang of disappointment. He wasn't going to be able to even the score with the nigga who shot him.

As he looked across the seat, disappointment turned to horror. From where he stood, he could see the driver already had the drop on Tamel. Before he could react, Killa heard the shot thundering, and saw Tamel take one point blank range in the chest.

"Shit!" he mumbled to himself.

Things were going from bad to worse. Killa stepped back and started dumping shots into the car. As Javon heard the shots coming from behind him, one grazed him. The next one hit him in the back, causing him to tumble out of the car. Though he was hit, he jumped up quickly, and started firing over the roof of the car. The dark-skinned shooter on the passenger side was already running. He was halfway across the street.

"Fatima, come on, hurry up!"

He reached in to give her a hand, and his whole world stood still. Fatima was slumped sideways in a puddle of blood with gunshot wounds in her neck and face.

"Fatima!" He screamed her name as he reached for her, hoping against what his eyes were telling him was obvious. "No! God, no! *Please* don't let her be dead!"

He tried to sit her up, but her head lolled to one side and she slumped over again. He felt the tears quickly escaping his eyes.

He stepped out of the car and sat on the curb, the weight of the gun heavy in his hand. He slumped his head and let the tears that were running down his face, and the gun in his hand, both fall to the ground.

Triple Crown Publications presents . . .

EPILOGUE | Fatima's death touched the world. Like the deaths of Aaliyah and Lisa Lopes before her, fans lined the streets across the nation to hold tributes to Fatima. In Africa, millions more mourned one of their own daughters, lost to the senseless violence. Stars of the music industry praised her talent. G-Rydah wrote a poignant rap song expressing his grief at the loss of his sister in the game.

The official news version called it a car jacking turned tragedy. The media described the urban violence that had stolen a young life so full of potential as a tragic loss to the music industry and to the world. Rumors of Fatima's ties to radical black underground elements gave rise to a number of conspiracy theories about her death.

Her body was flown back to Tanzania to be laid to rest with her mother. The funeral was attended by African dignitaries, the rich and famous, and her father. Fatima's CD flew off the shelf, taking an already platinum debut to near diamond status. In death, she had become the star she had always wanted to be.

Javon did not attend the funeral. He was out on bail for manslaughter charges in connection with the death of Tamel. Javon had the best legal team that money could buy, led by Johnny Cochran himself.

In all the media coverage given to Fatima's death, few noticed the death that followed hers. One in particular was given a few lines in the newspaper police blotter. "The body of a stripper,

Patricia Wells, was found in a lot in Hunts Point. She had been shot at close range." Though the police had no suspects in the case, the word on the streets was Derrick had taken care of it personally.

Derrick also learned the hit on him had been sent by Marria's brother, Raphael. Before her death, Marria had confided in her closest cousin about her affair with Derrick. Her cousin had shared the information with Raphael, and Raphael had come to believe that Derrick was behind the robbery and murder of Manny and Marria.

Two months after the hit on Derrick, his brother Erick was transferred to Marion. Soon thereafter, Raphael was found dead in his cell, with puncture wounds in his neck and chest.

In Brooklyn, the police were looking for Derrick to question him about two Hispanic men shot dead in East New York. However, no one knew where Derrick was. Some said he was down south hustling, while others said he was laying up in the Cayman Islands.

Two weeks after Fatima's funeral, Killa was seen hustling on the corner of Gates and Nostrand, when a black van crept up the block, and in broad daylight, four black men jumped out. They hit Killa with a stun gun, then threw him in the back of the van and drove away. No one knew who the men were and no one has seen or heard from Killa since. The only thing most who witnessed the event agreed on, was that the men were all wearing what looked to be black beads around their neck with funny looking crosses on them.

THE BLESSING OF LOVE COMES WITH
THE HONOR OF LOYALTY

ORDER FORM

Triple Crown Publications
PO Box 6888
Columbus, Oh 43205

Name: _____

Address: _____

City/State: _____

Zip: _____

TITLES	PRICES
Dime Piece	$15.00
Gangsta	$15.00
Let That Be The Reason	$15.00
A Hustler's Wife	$15.00
The Game	$15.00
Black	$15.00
Dollar Bill	$15.00
A Project Chick	$15.00
Road Dawgz	$15.00
Blinded	$15.00
Diva	$15.00
Sheisty	$15.00
Grimey	$15.00
Me & My Boyfriend	$15.00
Larceny	$15.00
Rage Times Fury	$15.00
A Hood Legend	$15.00
Flipside of The Game	$15.00
Menage's Way	$15.00

SHIPPING/HANDLING (Via U.S. Media Mail) $3.95 1-2 Books, $5.95 3-4 Books add $1.95 for ea. additional book

TOTAL $_____

FORMS OF ACCEPTED PAYMENTS:
Postage Stamps, Institutional Checks & Money Orders, all mail in orders take 5-7 Business days to be delivered.

ORDER FORM

Triple Crown Publications
PO Box 6888
Columbus, Oh 43205

ame: _____

ddress: _____

ity/State: _____

ip: _____

	TITLES	PRICES
	Still Sheisty	$15.00
	Chyna Black	$15.00
	Game Over	$15.00
	Cash Money	$15.00
	Crack Head	$15.00
	For The Strength of You	$15.00
	Down Chick	$15.00
	Dirty South	$15.00
	Cream	$15.00
	Hoodwinked	$15.00
	Bitch	$15.00
	Stacy	$15.00
	Life	$15.00
	Keisha	$15.00
	Mina's Joint	$15.00
	How To Succeed in The Publishing Game	$20.00
	Love & Loyalty	$15.00
	Whore	$15.00
	A Hustler's Son	$15.00

HIPPING/HANDLING (Via U.S. Media Mail) $3.95 1-2 Books, $5.95 3-4 Books add $1.95 for ea. additional book

TOTAL $_____

FORMS OF ACCEPTED PAYMENTS:
ostage Stamps, Institutional Checks & Money Orders, all mail in orders take 5-7 Business days to be delivered.

ORDER FORM

Triple Crown Publications
PO Box 6888
Columbus, Oh 43205

Name: _____

Address: _____

City/State: _____

Zip: _____

	TITLES	PRICES
	Chances	$15.00
	Contagious	$15.00
	Hold U Down	$15.00
	Black and Ugly	$15.00
	In Cahootz	$15.00
	Dirty Red *Hardcover Only*	$20.00
	Dangerous	$15.00
	Street Love	$15.00
	Sunshine & Rain	$15.00
	Bitch Reloaded	$15.00
	Dirty Red *Paperback*	$15.00
	Mistress of the Game	$15.00
	Queen	$15.00
	The Set Up	$15.00
	Torn	$15.00
	Stained Cotton	$15.00
	Grindin *Hardcover Only*	$10.00

SHIPPING/HANDLING (Via U.S. Media Mail) $3.95 1-2 Books, $5.95 3-4 Books add $1.95 for ea. additional book

TOTAL $_____

FORMS OF ACCEPTED PAYMENTS:
Postage Stamps, Institutional Checks & Money Orders, all mail in orders take 5-7 Business days to be delivered.

EAST ORANGE PUBLIC LIBRARY

3 2665 0037 4848 2

6/08

Mayer, Deborah.
Love & loyalty **DISCARD**

DATE DUE

MAR 1 7 2009		
JUN 0 3 2009		
FEB 1 7 2016		
FEB 2 3 2016		

GAYLORD   #3523PI   Printed in USA

AMPERE BRANCH